NARC

NARC

Crissa-Jean Chappell

Woodbury, Minnesota

First Edition
First Printing, 2012

Book design by Bob Gaul
Cover design by Lisa Novak
Cover image © Rod Morata/Stone/Getty Images
Editing by Nicole Edman

Flux, an imprint of Llewellyn Worldwide Ltd.

Library of Congress Cataloging-in-Publication Data
Chappell, Crissa-Jean.
    Narc/Crissa-Jean Chappell.—1st ed.
      p. cm.
    ISBN 978-0-7387-3247-3
    I. Title.
    PS3603.H3755N37 2012
    813'.6—dc23
                                            2011053171

Flux
Llewellyn Worldwide Ltd.
2143 Wooddale Drive
Woodbury, MN 55125-2989
www.fluxnow.com

Printed in the United States of America

For Joyce Sweeney,
And for all the Miami kids
from Kendall to Wynwood.

PART ONE

1 Off-site

The empty room was in Little Havana, above a botánica that sold life-sized statues of bleeding saints. My new "friend," the undercover cop, and I never met in the same place twice. We were supposed to talk off-site on a weekly basis, just to keep me in character.

The cop was dressed in regular clothes: a T-shirt and jeans, same as me, but his hair was buzzed so tight, you could see the pasty gleam of his scalp shining through it. He wanted to know if I'd been taking notes. So far, all I'd written down were a couple names from school.

"Aaron, this is the best you can do?" he snapped.

I hung my head.

If I could've backed out, I would. Believe me. I never wanted anything so badly. That's the damn truth. If I thought things were shitty in my old life, I had no idea how low I could go. I'd been coasting without a clue. Then came the Incident.

Here's how it went down.

The Incident, as I like to refer to it, took place a few weeks into my senior year, right after Dad died. I was driving his truck down US-1, the highway that runs through Miami and all the way to the Keys, blasting my music with my little sister, Haylie, riding shotgun. Just trying to clear my head, you know? I was probably going ten over the limit. Okay. Maybe twenty. I didn't mean to run the light. It was one of those situations where you're like, should I slow down or speed up?

"Punch it," my sister said.

I hit the gas.

The siren blended into the radio. I didn't hear it at first. In the rearview mirror, I caught the blue and red. My blood turned to ice. What the hell was I going to tell Mom? She had enough to handle. I swerved through traffic, as if I could actually shake the cop. How dumb was that? Next thing I know, he's pulling us over and tapping the window.

"How's it going, man?" he said.

How did he think it was going?

"Axl Rose, huh?" He fake-smiled at me.

I had no clue what he meant. Then I remembered to cut the radio. For a second, I actually believed that we'd bond over classic rock and he'd let me off with a warning. No dice.

"You got any ID?"

I reached for my wallet.

"Can you guys step out of the vehicle? Make it quick." He shined a flashlight in my sister's eyes. "Been drinking tonight?"

"She's only fourteen," I said. "Give her a break."

He made me lean over the trunk, legs splayed, hands flat, while he rummaged through my pockets.

"Got anything on you that's going to stick me?" he asked.

"Just a pocketknife."

The cop looked confused. He dug inside my back pocket and fished out a Swiss Army Knife, a gift from Dad. I don't know why I was carrying the damn thing. It had rusted years ago.

He turned to Haylie. "How about you, sweetie?" he said, grinning.

I wanted to smash that grin off his face.

As his fingers moved across my sister's jeans, I gritted my teeth.

"What's this?" He slipped his fingers in her waistband. I was about to explode when he pulled out a plastic baggie, a little over an ounce. I must've stared at it for ten seconds before my brain added up the details:

My little sister.

A bag of weed.

Her eyes widened.

She must've got it from me. Where else would she get her hands on pot? I'd stashed away the "funeral present" from my friend, Collin, just in case I needed it, but I sure as hell didn't need it then.

"How much you pay for this?" he asked.

"I found it," she said.

"You found it."

"Yeah."

"Sure you don't sell that?"

Haylie was crying now, silently, her face slicked with tears and snot.

"Then why is it all bundled for sale?"

She opened her mouth.

"It's mine," I said, before she could fill in the blank.

The cop studied my driver's license. "Hang tight. I'm going to run your name."

I waited for what felt like centuries. My heart was jackhammering. God, how could I be so stupid? When the cop finally came back, his mood had shifted.

"You're Rico's kid," he said. "I heard what happened overseas. Your father was a brave man."

"Yes," I said. "He was."

"How's your mom doing?"

"Not good."

The cop nodded. "That's your little sister? What's her name again?"

"Haylie."

"Haylie. Right."

If this cop was such good buddies with Dad, why couldn't he remember my sister's name? He told her to get in the truck. When she was gone, he edged closer to me.

"Tell you what," he said. "If you're straight with me ... Well. It all depends. Maybe we can work something out."

"I don't understand," I said, falling right into it.

"This is kind of serious. I could book her for possession of an illegal substance with intent to sell. Or you could go to jail. Looks like you're about to turn eighteen in a few weeks. What's it going to be?"

"I already told you. It's mine. Please. Just leave her alone, she's just a kid," I stammered.

If I went to jail, who would watch over Haylie? I glanced back at the truck.

"You go to school?" he asked.

"Yes, sir," I said like a little kid.

"Whereabouts?"

"Palm Hammock."

His mouth twitched. I could almost see his wheels turning.

"Since you seem cooperative, I'm willing to offer a deal. I'll dismiss the girl's charges if you'll work with me."

I was freaking, big time, ready to do anything.

"Do you know what the word *informant* means?" he asked. "It means a friend who helps us out. They supply information. We help them out in return."

The Barney theme song played in my head with new words:

I help you. You help me.

———————

On the way home, Haylie said, "I can't believe he just let us go."

"Dad's got friends in high places," I said. "Now start talking. What's with the weed? You're way too young to be messing with that shit."

She shrugged. "I found it in your room."

Right. I turned on the radio. For the rest of the drive, we kept quiet.

A few days later, I drove to the police station. The same cop ushered me into a windowless office in Narcotics, where the lead officer of the team leaned over the conference table and gave me a speech about my "assignment." Then they took my picture and fingerprinted me like a murderer.

There's a word for what they did. It's called *flipping*. In order to drop the marijuana charges, I had to become a new person: Metro Dade Informant Number 2012-1003. The lead officer logged me into the system. He did a background check, pulled my history, and gave me a brand-new file.

"Aren't you supposed to get permission from my mom or something?" I asked.

"You're almost eighteen, right? So we're treating you

like an emancipated adult," he said, and I liked the way it sounded. Emancipated. Free.

When the cops asked if I was willing to sign the Substantial Assistance Agreement and go undercover, I said, "Okay," and just like that, I had a new job, one that I couldn't discuss with anybody.

The subject of my assignment? The same place I'd been going since ninth grade: Palm Hammock in West Kendall. For years, my school had been dodging phone calls from angry parents, desperate to shake its reputation as "the pharmacy." The cops weren't interested in setting up the school for a drug bust. They had one goal: catch the shot caller in action. After targeting the head dealer, I was supposed to alert the lead officer, who would call in the troops for an arrest.

I wouldn't call myself a party person, yet the cop was ordering me to hang with anyone who might have connections to the shot caller. In other words, the cool kids, not the stoner rejects like me at the bottom of the social totem pole.

This meant going to parties.

This meant making friends.

And another problem: They had to be the right ones.

2 Aaron With Two As

I've been in trouble lots of times, but never on purpose. The morning after my useless check-in with the cop, I sat in World History, doodling pot leaves on my desk. I made sure that people noticed. That was the plan. My doodles sent a message: *Let's get high.* So far nobody had taken the bait. Then Mr. Pitstick noticed what I was doing and gave me a lunch detention for "destroying school property." When lunchtime finally rolled around, I ate my turkey sandwich in the classroom with the other convicts.

Time to take notes.

Somebody's cell phone buzzed, the ring tone featuring the classic strains of *I'm In Love With a Stripper.* It belonged to Jessica Torres, better known as Skully, a redhead with a reverse mullet (party in the front, business in the back).

She tried to lower the volume, making a bloop-bloop noise with every push of the button.

"Call you later," she whispered.

Unbelievable. Who talks on their cell during detention? I couldn't get over it. Neither could Mr. Pitstick, who was already marching down the aisle.

Skully dipped lower at her desk, as if that did any good. "Listen, dingle-brain. You have to check it three times a day. Did you eat candy again? What the hell is wrong with you? Do it yourself. Use the flash lancing thingie. Yeah. The one with the see-through cap."

Mr. Pitstick snatched the phone out of her grip. He snapped it shut and tucked it into his pocket. "Ms. Torres, cellular phones are not allowed on school grounds." He strutted toward the front of the classroom.

Skully actually got up and followed him. "Hear me out," she said. "My little brother locked himself out of the house and he needs his meds. No one else is there. He's got diabetes."

"Rules are rules."

"Yeah, but the rule sucks. Say there's an accident. What happens if the school burns down or something?"

The class rocked with laughter.

"Settle, people," said Mr. Pitstick. The cell phone went off again, triggering another round of shrieks and giggles. He walked back to his desk and tossed the phone in a drawer.

Skully was upset, almost in tears. I kind of felt bad for her. "I swear to god it's an emergency."

Mr. Pitstick sank into his chair. He's got this holier-than-thou smirk that I really can't stand. So I did something stupid.

I raised my hand.

"Maybe she's telling the truth," I heard myself say. "I just don't think it's fair, taking away her phone."

Heads turned to gawk at me. A few people whispered.

For a long time, Mr. Pitstick stayed quiet. Then he shrugged. "Who said life was fair?"

Everybody leaned toward me, waiting for a showdown, waiting for me to do something. Anything. Instead, I did nothing, as usual, and they went back to chewing their pencils.

———

It was raining in the library. The sharp tang of mold hit me as I pushed through the double doors. Last summer's hurricane had ripped the stuffing out of the roof. Around the room, water plinked into buckets. Half the books got tossed, not that anyone came here to read. This was the only safe zone I knew. A place where I could think. I cruised the magazine rack and pretended to read about oil spills. The librarian, a middle-aged dude with a straggly ponytail, hunched at his desk, playing a game of solitaire. Kind of pathetic. But not as lame as me.

I kept looking up people online, like some kind of inept cyber-stalker. For a while I tried using "Palm Hammock" as a search on Facebook, but I didn't see anyone familiar. The only person I recognized from school was this cute, emo-looking girl named Morgan Baskin. We were in the same history class but we never talked. Not like I'd ever tried; she was far too cool for me.

I switched back to Morgan's Facebook page. The first thing I noticed is how lonely it looked. When I clicked on photos, I found a Polaroid of a bare arm, crisscrossed with scars. The marks were thin and raised like an ice skater's trail on a frozen lake. I felt embarrassed just looking at it, like I was peeping on her.

The people in her friends list didn't go to Palm Hammock. They were from all over the planet, from Australia to Iceland. I scanned through her only blog entry: Everybody Is So Fake. There's No One Left Who's Real.

> *i grab the blade and carve*
> *this skin which no longer feels*
> *normal*
> *drowning in those faces*
> *who try to catch me*
> *the current's just too strong.*

For some reason, I couldn't stop reading it. Guess you could say I was spacing out. I'm not big into poetry, but there was something between the words that made total sense. My eighth grade English teacher, Mrs. Scoggins, would've called it an epiphany.

Not for the first time, I was beginning to have doubts

about this assignment. What right did I have to be prying into people's lives? I felt like an asshole.

The library door opened and a bunch of people headed straight for the so-called "lounge" near the computers. I quickly minimized my screen and cleared the search history.

Brent Campbell sprawled across a table with Morgan, the emo-looking girl I had just been checking out online. They used to go out for, like, half a second. Not that I keep track of stuff like that. No telling if they were back together, but Morgan deserved better, if you asked me. Besides. She was way too cute.

Her bangs fell across her face like a shadow. She had a lip ring and a million hoops glinting along her earlobes. I could picture her at a Renaissance fair, selling dreamcatchers or jars marked "ashes of evil fairies."

Morgan liked to tell everyone that she danced ballet professionally. I believed it. Her muscular legs nearly stretched the length of the table. She always wore flat shoes—moccasins or pillowy Uggs trimmed with fake fur. She must've been sweating in those boots because she kicked them under her chair. Until then, I'd never seen her bare toes. They were thick with calluses, almost bent the wrong way.

"Oh, my god. That boy is staring at my feet. What a pervert," she said, pointing at me.

Brent turned so fast, he might've got whiplash. A trio of studs glinted across his pointy chin, as if a nail gun had attacked him. Right. Like that's so hardcore. "Got a problem?"

"Not really," I said.

"Leave him alone," Morgan said. "I can't blame him for staring. My toes are fugly. They're totally messed up from jumping in pointe shoes." She rolled her eyes. "Hey, did you know I danced in a commercial?"

"Yeah," I said.

Morgan looked surprised. "You do?"

"She was, like, ten," Brent said.

"Shut up." She gave me a little smack. "So, like...how do you know?"

"Everybody does," I said. "It's online."

"Really?" she said.

"Somebody uploaded it," Brent told her, as if she didn't already know. She's probably the one who put it there.

In the milk commercial, Morgan wore pigtails and fake eyelashes.

"Does a body good!" she sang, a catchphrase that would never die, thanks to the video posted on YouTube, not to mention the boys who chanted it whenever she walked down the hall.

Brent ripped a page from his notebook. He was always working on some dumbass rap lyric, spitting out rhymes about hustling and hos. If he didn't make it to the major leagues, he was going to play out his beef in freestyle battles. "It's good to have a backup plan," I once overheard him say.

"Your boobs are popping through your shirt," he told Morgan, holding up her drawing. "You can see the nipples and everything. Were you smoking when you drew this?"

My ears perked up at what might be my first lead.

"I refuse to answer that question," she muttered. An answer in itself.

I'd never seen Morgan Baskin at the Tombstone, this spot on the edge of campus where the smokers hung out with their pipes and rolling papers. The Tombstone was just a stupid block of fake marble bombed with bird poop. It had a bunch of rich people's names carved into it, including some kid who died back when I was a freshman.

I didn't really know the dead guy. He was a few years ahead of me. Someone said that his girlfriend had just dumped him. All I could remember was the bandanna he wore all the time. On the day of his memorial, his locker was plastered with cards. The school put his picture on a music stand in the auditorium. A couple people stood and mumbled into the microphone. His girlfriend talked about how much he loved Egg McMuffins. When I'm dead, I hope that somebody remembers more than just my favorite fast food.

They said the guy had a big heart. They didn't talk about his bad grades. They didn't mention the car crash, the six pack of beer, or fight with his ex. Maybe dying isn't so bad, if people remember who they want you to be rather than what you were.

The Tombstone wasn't Morgan's scene. We were at

opposite ends of the social scale, so that made sense. But that didn't necessarily mean she wasn't interested in weed. Now was the time to make a move. Only one problem: I had no idea what to do or say around this girl.

"So. Skully's house party. Are we going or not?" she asked Brent.

Skully's parties were the stuff of legend. Of course, I had never actually been to any of them.

"I'm going," I said, taking a seat at their table.

Brent thumped my arm. "Who are you?"

Morgan grinned. "God. You sound like a Nazi. That's Aaron Foster." She leaned forward and her shirt dipped open, flashing a glimpse of "the puppies," as Collin used to call them. I tried to focus on a strip of masking tape on the carpet.

"You know my name?"

"Of course. You're the enemy," she said, keeping her gaze locked on mine. Was she onto me? What the hell was that supposed to mean? At that moment, I imagined her mind scanning me, trying to fit me into the right slot. I was the "quiet kid," so quiet that teachers skipped over my name while taking attendance. In other words, I was human wallpaper.

Brent meanwhile was going off about Photoshop, how digital cameras had "replaced drawing as an art form." Did he really think he was impressing her with his amazing intellect? Anyway, I was no expert on what girls wanted to hear.

"Whatever, Brent," Morgan said. "I'm still going to take Advanced Drawing next semester."

"My dad was a photographer for the Air Force," I told her. "He used to take these really dramatic pictures of things like soldiers jogging in a sandstorm. You know. *National Geographic* stuff."

"Where is he now?"

I didn't answer.

"Oh." Morgan stared at her fingernails. After a minute, she said, "You're a military brat?"

I told her my first lie. "I was born on a base in the Azores, these little islands off Portugal." Actually, I've never been out of the country. I just looked at my dad's photos. God. This whole lying thing was getting easier. That's the part that freaked me out.

"So that makes you an alien," said Brent.

Morgan tapped my arm, and I could feel my skin burning. "What was it like there?" she wanted to know.

"Pretty weird. My parents used to play golf near this extinct volcano. The sand on the beaches was black."

"That's so amazing," she said, touching me again.

At this point, Brent was about to explode. "Why are you flirting with this dude?" He scooted closer, as if to kiss her, but she moved. Instead, he licked her cheek.

"Gross," she said, pushing him away.

He picked up Morgan's sketchbook and flipped through it. "Why don't you rip out these pages?" He tossed it across the table. "You should stick to taking crappy photos."

"Let me do it over," she said, lunging for the sketchpad.

He yanked it away. "You only draw skulls and shit. That's the problem. Get a magic marker and make the neckline thicker. Make the shading a little more...you know. What the hell were you thinking?"

I studied the drawing. Maybe it was supposed to be a self-portrait. It looked nothing like her blunt little face. The proportions were all wrong. Obviously, the girl was a fan of anime. The only thing she got right was the hair, which looked like a Cleopatra wig, dark and angular.

Morgan made a big deal about gathering her pencils. On her way out she slammed the door so hard, it rattled.

The librarian didn't seem to care. He was already back at his desk, shuffling cards, rearranging hearts and spades as if the order of the universe depended on it. I wanted to tell him that it must be tough, working in a place where you're considered the bad guy just for doing your job.

That's something I could relate to.

I grabbed my stuff, making sure to fetch Morgan's drawing from the trash on the way out.

———

Class had ended hours ago, but I didn't feel like going home yet. I kept drifting around the campus. Palm Hammock is one of those "al fresco" schools where the classrooms are spaced between sunny breezeways. I was halfway down the steps when I decided to turn back to Pitstick's classroom.

19

I jiggled the handle, but it didn't budge. The lock, however, looked ancient. After a quick scan of the hall, making sure it was clear, I plucked a safety pin off my messenger bag. All it took was one twist. The door swung on its hinges, and I snuck inside.

Mr. Pitstick had swept everything off his desk, including his coffee cup, which left a trail of stains, little tree-ring circles in the upper right corner. Weird. The drawer didn't have a lock. I slid it open and found Skully's rhinestone-studded cell phone on top of a pile of dry-erase markers.

I flipped the cell open. The battery was near death, but I quickly scrolled through the list of names and numbers, trying to make sense of them.

Ace, Bubba, Charro, JJ, Skye, YoYo

Skully's so-called friends. Did she even know their last names? I gave up and threw the cell in my bag.

As I hustled out of the classroom, I was moving so fast I didn't even notice Skully lurking in the hall. In fact, I almost tripped over her.

"Watch where you're going," she said, pushing me away. Her eyes flashed over me. "I've seen you around. What's your name again?"

"Aaron."

"With two a's?"

"Yeah."

"That's the worst kind," she said. "Don't worry, though. I won't judge you."

From my bag, the cell phone rang. Her cell phone.

Skully blinked.

I wiped my sweaty palms on my pants and dug out Skully's phone. "I believe this is yours," I said, handing it to her.

"Holy shit," she said, snatching it away. "You did not steal that back for me."

"Okay. I didn't."

As if on cue, the cell phone rang again. We both cracked up. Skully's smile faded as soon as she answered it.

"That's insane," she muttered into the phone. "You can't use it now. Throw it in the trash." She hung up and said, "He left his insulin bottle in the closet. I told him to put it in the fridge, but he keeps forgetting on purpose."

"That sucks," I said.

Skully pulled out a carton of slim brown Indian cigarettes. "Ever smoke bidis? I get them from this crazy health food store in the Grove." She snapped her lighter, but it wouldn't spark. "Damn it. You wouldn't happen to have a light? I mean, you kind of look like a smoker."

"What's a smoker look like?" I asked, a little offended.

She shrugged. "I don't know. That wasn't an insult, by the way."

I grabbed a box of matches from my bag. When I opened it, I pretended to act all irritated. "Why do I always put the used ones back?"

"I do that, too," Skully said. Actually, I had colored the burnt-looking tips with black marker. Her eyes almost popped out of her head when I struck the "used" match and it ignited. Just like magic.

"You got special powers or something?" she asked.

If only. Then I could've zapped away all the guilt I felt about faking this whole conversation.

Skully put two bidis in her mouth and lit them at the same time. When she handed mine over, it was still damp. We were outside, but smoking was still off limits on school grounds. Not that I cared.

"They say these are really bad for you. Like, worse than regular tobacco."

"Whatever," she said. "I don't smoke cigarettes."

"Then what do you smoke?" I asked. She just giggled.

As we walked down the breezeway, I tried to think of something else to say. "So how long you been stuck at Palm Hammock?"

"It's a life sentence," she said. The bidi dangled from her lips, bobbing with the rhythm of her words. "I've been here since my paste-eating days. You have no idea how much it sucks. I mean, if I switched schools, I could totally reinvent myself."

I blew out a stream of smoke. "You know a lot of people at Palm Hammock?"

"Who told you that?" she asked.

"Nobody. I just figured. Since you've been here so long."

"Don't remind me." Skully smiled. Although it was, like, a hundred degrees outside, she was wearing these checkered arm warmers, which she rolled up and down.

"Excuse me, ladies," said Mr. Pitstick, hustling around the lockers. You could spot him from twenty feet away. He wore a bike helmet clamped over his head like a Day-Glo walnut. I turned around and he smirked. "I mean lady and gentleman."

Just then Skully's cell phone went off again. It was so damn loud, there was no question where it came from.

Mr. Pitstick stared at us. I waited for him to mention the phone. Instead, he said, "No smoking on campus."

My bidi had burned to ashes anyway, so I just tossed it in the bushes.

He wagged a finger at Skully. "Put it out, Ms. Torres."

She flicked her bidi on the ground and smushed it with her Godzilla-sized boots. "God. He must be deaf or something. What's wrong with him?" she said as he walked away. "Besides his love affair with booze. I bet you've already heard about his brush with death last Christmas. He crashed his car into a telephone pole, lost his license and everything."

Geez. This girl was a walking Wikipedia.

"That's intense," I said, watching Mr. Pitstick unlock his bike, an old-school Huffy dappled with rust.

"I'm surprised he's still alive," Skully said. "Thanks again for rescuing my phone. Mr. Pitstick is an ass. It's like, he doesn't realize there might be a good reason why I'm breaking the rules. I have a life, you know?"

"Exactly," I said.

She nodded once, then skipped off like a grade-schooler.

The back of her head was pale white with pink streaks. It reminded me of fur, like a stuffed animal. When she was gone, I whipped out my memo pad and added her name to my list.

3 Solitaire

The breeze smelled like cut grass and leftover thunderstorms. I made my way to the Tombstone. A bunch of people were hanging out there, including Nolan Struth, this kid that everybody liked to torture, just for the hell of it.

Nolan was in the Special Needs program. He was never going to graduate, in any real sense of the word. Every year, he racked up useless classes like Video Production. During the morning announcements, he rolled his wheelchair in front of the camera and read the list of vegetarian lunch options. That was his big thing, along with his never-ending science experiments.

"How's the time machine coming along?" I asked him.

"Still working on it," he said. "Needs more plutonium.

And that's kind of hard to find, unless you know the right sources."

The guys started tearing into him, saying stuff like, "Hey, Nolan! Can I borrow your time machine?"

"Well, you would have to get on the waiting list…" he said, ultraserious. Nolan wasn't stupid. He just wanted to be there so bad that he put up with their shit.

If I had a time machine, I would zoom into the future, then float back in time and get things right.

I took a walk around the empty football field to clear my head. I needed to meet people if I was going to find the shot caller. At the same time, it was kinda nice talking to girls. At school, I hardly talked to anyone, didn't have any friends. Of course, this was all going to hit the fan, sooner or later, and I wouldn't have friends then either. Why did I care what they thought of me? I should stop caring.

There was Morgan, sitting alone on the bleachers. Just like that, the lights around the goal posts clicked on. I was bathed in fluorescence, like I was going to recite poetry or something. Instead, I climbed up and found a spot a few seats down from her.

"Hey," I called out.

Morgan didn't hear me. She was too busy fiddling with her old-school iPod, scrolling that stupid wheel around with her thumb. Instead of ear buds, she had these enormous Walkman-style headphones that would've kept her warm in a blizzard. Maybe if I stared long enough, she would feel it.

She bopped her head to the beat. In her other hand, she gripped something sharp and metallic. It looked like a piece of aluminum screening, the kind that shelters swimming pools. I watched her lift up her skirt and drag the metal across the pale flesh of her inner thigh. She did this a couple more times, slow, careful strokes, then slipped the piece of metal in her sock.

I sucked in a gulp. For the past few seconds, I'd forgotten to breathe. Morgan was looking at me now. After a second, she unplugged herself from the headphones.

I could see her eyes now, which were puffy from crying. I thought about walking away. Too late. She'd already noticed me. I moved closer instead.

"Are you a spy?" she asked.

"You mean like James Bond?" I tried to concentrate on walking.

"There was this book I was obsessed with as a little kid. This girl, Harriet, goes around spying on everyone. When the people at her school find out, they end up hating her for telling the truth."

"What's your name again?" I asked, like I didn't remember.

"Morgan Baskin. Like the ice cream company. Not that I'm related."

"You never know. Maybe they're the long-lost branches of your family tree."

"I wish," she rolled her eyes. "Then I'd be set for life. Unfortunately, my family tree is suffering from root rot."

I laughed. This girl was so crush-worthy. Why the hell was she talking to me?

"We're in the same history class, right?" she said. "Mr. Pitstick?"

"That's right. He busted me today."

"For what? Cheating on that quiz about the Trojan War? For the record, everybody did. Brent sent me the answers on his cell phone."

"No, I actually studied for that. But I got in trouble for doodling."

"Geez. He should've locked you up in Supermax. I bet you'd look good in an orange jumpsuit."

Look good? What did she mean? Was she flirting with me? This felt so wrong. I needed to stop obsessing.

"I doubt it," I told her. "Orange isn't my color."

"Is it anyone's?" asked Morgan. She slung her bag across her chest.

"You're left-handed."

"Yep. But my stepmom made me use my other hand. She used to tie a rubber band around my wrist and snap it when I used my left."

Hearing that was like getting kicked in the guts, as if her pain had leaked into my skin.

"That really sucks," I said.

"It's no big deal. Now I'm ambidextrous," Morgan said. "Most of the world's famous artists were left-handed, you know. Like Michelangelo."

"The ancient Greeks thought it was unlucky."

"Gee. Thanks." She blew the bangs off her face. Up close, she was smaller than I realized, half-drowning in her granny-style getup. When she spoke, her gravelly voice poured out so slow and deep, it surprised me.

"You smoke?" Morgan took out a pack of rolling papers, along with a pouch of tobacco.

"Not cigarettes," I said slowly.

"Gotcha," she said, sticking out her tongue and licking the end of a sheet. "You looking for bud?"

"Yeah."

"How much do you need?"

"A dime bag," I told her, "for the weekend."

"Talk to Jessica. She'll hook you up." Morgan plugged herself into the headphones. Screamy music leaked out.

"Jessica?" I asked, a little confused. I kept flashing back to Morgan's skin, those cuts, her skirt bunched above her thighs. It was getting hard to concentrate.

"Hello? Jessica Torres? Otherwise known as Skully?"

"Oh, right," I said. "You're going to that thing on Saturday, right?"

"Maybe," she said.

It took her a minute to juggle her bag, an army medic knapsack decorated with a cross, and rip a page out of her Health book. "Give me your back."

"Um. Okay."

She mashed the paper against my shoulder blade. The sharp tip of her pen skittered up and down. "I'm done now," she said.

I turned around and saw her folding the note into an origami flower.

"Here you go," she said, handing it to me.

Between a paragraph on CPR *("Perform abdominal thrusts until foreign body expels...")* she had scribbled a row of digits, along with her name. I noticed that she dotted the *i* in Baskin with a heart.

Morgan took her time, walking to the bottom of the bleachers. There was a bike in the grass, the handlebars looped with duct tape.

"I'm out like sauerkraut," she said, swinging her leg over the bike's front bar, no easy feat in that boho getup—a skirt that looked like something my grandma would drape over her kitchen window. Morgan was one of those girls who never look young, then grow up and never look old.

"Take it easy," I waved.

She pushed off and glided into the street, her bike tick-tick-ticking like it was about to blow up. I stood there, watching her grow smaller and smaller, until she dipped into the street and slid into traffic, going the wrong way against the cars.

When she was gone, I whipped out my memo pad. I wrote, "MORGAN." Then I drew a star next to her name.

———

Status: UNSENT
To: LadyM
From: Metroid
Subject: Wake Me Up When September Ends

Dear Morgan,

When I saw you on the bleachers, I thought you looked like Cleopatra. (Obviously, I've been watching too much History Channel. I caught this show where a bunch of archeologists dug up some Roman coins with her face carved on them. She looked really different from the movies. Actually, she wasn't that hot).

Okay. That sounded weird. Let's start over.

I'm sitting here in the basement laundry room. I keep thinking about last Friday in the library. I couldn't believe you were actually talking to me. Seriously. You and your friends are like royalty at Palm Hammock, and I'm this nonexistent entity. Guess that makes me the perfect spy.

You're going to hate me forever when you figure out what I'm really doing talking to you guys.

Then yesterday at the field, I started having second thoughts. You looked so cute, with your old-school headphones and that awesome dress. I mean, who wears a dress to school? I felt like you were being totally real with me. That was the best conversation I've had in months. To be honest, I used to think you were stuck up. (Not that I'm judging you or anything! Just saying!)

Notice I keep using exclamation points!!!!

I can't stop thinking about the stuff you said. Please don't think I'm a creeper. (I found your e-mail on fb.) I want to ask you a million stupid things. Question Numero Uno: Why were you hurting yourself?

I hold my cards close to the chest. Maybe you're like that, too.

I don't want you to get hurt, even if you are involved in this drug stuff.

I want you to understand that I'm working on a plan. Not sure what exactly. You can bet it won't be some lameass hero bullshit. I need to figure out a way to separate the good guys from the bad. And right now, that's not so easy. I mean, helping me find one bag of weed doesn't make you public enemy number one, does it?

My mom just came in here and yelled at me. I swear, she thinks I'm mentally damaged and can't function on my own.

This e-mail is becoming unintelligible. Sorry I'm not making any sense. I smoked a blunt and I'm decently baked.

I don't have the balls to send this letter.

I should sign it "sincerely," but that never sounds sincere.

—A.

4 Nothing To Wear

On Saturday morning, I practiced my magic. I'd been working on the ultimate trick—levitation. So far, I couldn't pull it off. I had to secretly balance on my toes, lifting myself a few inches off the ground. I tried it once in front of my little sister and fell on my ass. After a while, I just gave up.

Time to get to work.

I logged online and started Googling the names of people from school, plus the names on my list. Outside my window, the pigeons rustled and paced. I tugged back the drapes and saw a bird speckled like a cookie. I had named her Wendy, after the fast food joint that blinked across Biscayne Boulevard. In the flowerbox, she left a bunch of smooth, leathery eggs. Sometimes she disappeared for days. Just when I'd start to get worried, she'd fly home again.

Me and my mom and sister had been living in this shitty one-bedroom apartment since Dad died. We had to move out of our house, near the Air Force Base in Homestead, to a cheap apartment in downtown Miami. Mom and Haylie shared the bedroom. My sister never stopped complaining about it. She was lucky. I got stuck sleeping on a Murphy bed in the middle of the spider-infested living room.

In Homestead, it was all fields and farms. In downtown Miami, we were surrounded by fast food chains and motels with names like Seven Seas (although there was no sea in sight). I used to pass the same dead dog, sprawled at the exit for I-95, its face locked in a toothy snarl. It rotted there for days.

Mom was barely functioning. She was finishing up her nursing degree and spent most of her time working at South Miami Hospital, taking care of strangers, while I stayed home with Haylie. We watched endless marathons of the Marx Brothers and lived off Ritz crackers. I helped her figure out her activity sheets on quadratic equations and forged Mom's signature where it said, PARENT/GUARDIAN.

Haylie refused to believe that Dad wasn't coming home. Maybe that's because he hadn't been overseas long, then bam. We got hit with the news.

The soldiers appeared on our front step on a Saturday

morning. It was just after Dad had left for another photo assignment. He was never home long.

Haylie was still in her pajamas, watching the Cartoon Network, while I munched leftover pizza for breakfast. I joked that she was getting too old for superheroes, but we always watched TV together. Mom was snoring in the back bedroom. She had just finished another late shift at the hospital. She hadn't even taken off her scrubs, which I remember were decorated with tiny teddy bears.

Haylie ran to the door. Two men in uniform stood there—a chaplain and a sergeant. Both of them were drenched with sweat.

My sister knew. She started crying, and as I stumbled through the house, all the noises faded away, as if I'd floated into outer space, where sound doesn't exist: the stupid, high-pitched giggles on TV, the dog yapping as if demon-possessed, the dishwasher churning because I forgot to set it last night. All silent.

When I finally shook Mom awake, I didn't have to explain.

"They're here," I said.

She shot out of bed so fast, she knocked over a lamp. I tilted it upright and plugged it back into the wall. What the hell was I doing? I didn't want to go back out there. I already knew what the chaplain was going to say:

"The secretary of defense regrets to inform you … "

They muttered the words *cardiac arrest*, just a fancy way of saying that Dad's heart gave out. I couldn't even imagine it. In my mind, I envisioned Dad charging across the desert with a camera around his neck. Maybe he was shielding his buddies from an IED. Or maybe he was taking aerial pictures from a plane that crashed over enemy territory. I replayed these images over and over, fast-forwarding and rewinding. None of them were what really happened.

If I couldn't deal with the truth, I'd settle for something fake.

I kept poking around online, trying to find information about Skully's party—the one that I was supposedly crashing without an invite. It didn't take long to find her Facebook page, along with 1,490 of her closest "friends." Skully had posted an event:

> Full Moon Madness @ mi casa.
> Bring snax, booze, whatever/whomever u want.
>
> Here's the deal. I want to see ALL your beautiful faces.
> If u don't show up I will never talk to u again. JUST
> KIDDING!!!! LOL.

I scanned down the page. No address. Maybe somebody else had the details? It took me, like, half a century just to scan through her invite list. Under the names of people who had responded YES, I found Brent Campbell. I clicked over to his profile, where he had uploaded a picture of Lil Wayne, along with some weird lyric about Martians. Under this profound statement was a column of quizzes. Brent's answers stretched on for pages. Obviously, he had a lot of time on his hands. Among the highlights:

> In the past month have you Drank Alcohol? HELL
> YEAH. Your weakness? CASH AND THE LADIES.
> First thought waking up? GOTTA PISS.

I clicked back to his main page. Morgan was in his Top Friends. God. What was she doing with that tool? In the chat box, it said, *Online now!*

Here was my chance. I slid my finger over the keyboard, but I couldn't make a move. I was stuck on pause, just staring at the screen like a fool. How lame is that? Finally I sent an instant message (hi) and held my breath.

Seconds slid by.

Either she was ignoring me or away from the computer. *Please, please, please.*

My little sister barged into the room. She was holding our dog, Zeus, like a baby, and talking to him in this goofy voice: "Do you want to visit the doggy salon and get a mani-pedi? Yes? I think you need a makeover." She peered over my shoulder. "What are you doing? Looking at porn?"

"Nosy much?" I closed the screen. "Just checking my stocks."

Haylie dropped the dog into my lap. "Get off the computer. I need to borrow it."

"Nice. You practically threw him at me." I reached

down and massaged his wrinkles. Zeus licked my bare toes (Mom had a no-shoes policy in the apartment).

"He's all anorexic now," I told Haylie. "I mean, he has, like, no hair."

She snorted. "That's all kinds of wrong. Have you seen Mom?"

"Negative."

"Tell her I'm staying at a friend's house tonight."

"Where?"

"Now who's nosy?" she yelled, almost startling me out of my skin. God, she could be really annoying sometimes. She was silent for a moment, then she was making the dog "wave" at me, like nothing happened. "How come we never talk anymore?"

"That's not true, we talk," I told her. "I've just been really busy."

"With what?"

I glanced out the window. Mama Pigeon, Wendy, looked back at me, her eyes like drops of blood. She didn't move, not even when I tapped the glass and looked back at my sister.

"So what's new in the Life of Haylie?" I asked.

She rambled on about a boy who got suspended for bringing aspirin to school, the lack of dessert options in the lunchroom, and her creepy Health teacher, Mr. Mitchell.

"If you've got a headache," she said, "he'll sneak up behind you and rub your thumb. It's so weird."

"You mean, like acupressure?" I asked, glancing at the

laptop. I clicked back on the page, where an instant message blinked on the screen.

"I guess," said Haylie. "It's just plain gross, if you ask me."

"I didn't. Hey. Can we have this conversation later?" I scooted closer to my desk. The computer had gone blank. I'd left it alone too long. I pushed the space bar and the screen woke up again. There was an instant message reply on the screen, and it was from Morgan.

BRB

In other words, Be right back.

"If I tell you something, will you promise not to blab it all over the universe?" Haylie asked.

"Maybe."

"I've been hanging with this guy," she said.

"What guy? What do you mean 'hanging'? You're only in junior high. You're not old enough to date."

"Oh, my god. People at my school have been dating since, like, sixth grade. You promised not to tell."

"Okay, okay," I said.

"At least I have a social life. Unlike my stupid brother," she said, pushing my shoulder. "Can I use the computer now?"

"Not if you continue to insult me."

"Fine. Me and Zeus have better things to do," she said, scooping up the dog. She grabbed his leash and stomped out of the apartment.

My sister had no clue what was going on, despite the

fact that she was technically the whole point of this circus act. Her biggest problem was choosing between rainbow sprinkles or gummy worms at Whip 'n Dip.

Lucky.

The bathroom door banged open. Mom came rushing out, decked in her teddy bear scrubs.

"Haylie just took off," I told her. "She's staying at a friend's."

"What friend?"

"God. How do I know?"

Mom said, "I was clearing out your stuff when I noticed that you left your glasses in the closet. Don't you need them anymore?"

"Not really. The prescription is out of date. Besides...I prefer contacts."

"Well, you've got to give your eyes a rest sometime."

"That's okay, thanks."

"But you look so handsome with them on," she said.

"Actually, I don't."

Mom sighed. "If you damage your eyes, it's your own fault."

I stared at the computer screen, watching the cursor blink in 4/4 time. Almost as if I'd willed it to happen, up popped another instant message from Morgan.

I like iChat better. Can you log on?

Okay. I clicked the icon at the bottom of the screen, a

talk balloon from a comic book. Morgan IMed me at my listed screen name right away.

> LadyM: I will refrain from using the phrase 'what's up' cuz i use it too much and now i must atone.

I sat there, trying to think of what to say, but Mom wouldn't stop bugging me about the merits of wearing glasses. I tuned her out and started typing:

> Metroid: Sorry i'm not responsive … talking to Mom.
>
> LadyM: No prob. Are you coming to Skully's thing tonight? Should be memorable and destructive.
>
> Metroid: Yes. I might need a ride, tho.

Mom's voice screeched down the hall. "Are you on the computer? I can hear you pecking on the keyboard. It's very rude when someone's trying to talk to you, mister."

"Geez, Mom. Don't be so passive-aggressive. So what's the deal with Haylie? Is she still having nightmares?"

"Your sister is fine," Mom snapped.

Ever since Dad died, Haylie had been acting majorly weird. She distracted her brain with technology, vegging in front of the TV, just curled up in the blue glow. Mom tried to monitor our computer time for a while, but Haylie pitched a fit about it. Eventually, my sister got her way.

"Haylie keeps having nightmares," Mom said, "because she stays up late, watching those Japanese cartoons with all the blood and guts."

"Well, maybe if she wasn't left alone so much, she wouldn't watch that crap," I said. "She's only fourteen."

"What do you want me to do?" Her voice rose a notch. "I arranged my shifts at the hospital so I can be home in the morning."

"Whatever."

"I'm doing the best I can, Aaron. It might help if you talked to her more often. That goes for me, too. You only talk when you want something."

"Mom, please." I felt like I was trapped in my own personal rerun, the same conversation repeating over and over.

"How are you doing ... really?" she asked.

"Cool. Everything is cool."

She knew nothing about my life.

"All right then," she said and shook her head. "Talk to you later."

Mom always got the last word. When she finally left, I waited until the door shut and I could breathe steady again. Then I checked the computer. Morgan had sent me an IM so slangy, it should've come with a decoder ring.

WTF? Bummmmer. Wots up w/ ur wheelz?

I smiled, even though she couldn't see me. Why bother typing a *z* instead of an *s*? Does it really take that much longer to move your finger over to the *s* key?

Mom needs it for work tonight.

Which was the truth. I couldn't expect Morgan to offer

me a lift on her dilapidated bike, but she offered something better:

Let me pick u up. Where do u live?

Crap. No way could let her see our place. I needed to lie my way out of this. If I asked her to pick me up at school, she'd wonder how I got there. Technically, I wasn't supposed to be attending Palm Hammock anymore, but Mom lied about our address. I guess being a good liar is in my genes.

Metroid: I'm taking the Metrorail. Thanx!

LadyM: Kewl. See u at the Library?

Metroid: ???

LadyM: It's across from Dadeland Station.

Metroid: Library=the bookstore?

LadyM: Basically, yes.

Metroid: I see your logic.

LadyM: BTW... wot r u wearing? ;)

Metroid: Don't know yet. Maybe nothing.

LadyM: Naked=good. Haha. Peace out. (((((((((()))))))))))

Morgan signed off. I couldn't get over her offering me a ride, and the naked comment. This never would've happened last year. The only party invites I got were spam: *"Greetings. I looking for honest relations with loyal man..."*

To Morgan, I was still a mystery.

How long could it last?

I opened my closet and jangled the hangers. Back in junior high, I used to dress so sickeningly preppy. It was laughable, once you thought about it. People made fun of me because my shirts matched my socks. Everything matched. Even my underwear matched, just in case I got hit by a car or something and ended up in the hospital. That sure changed when we moved to Miami.

I settled on my old-school kicks, oversized hoodie, and ripped jeans. I'd worn these faded Levis so often, there was a hole in the left pocket. No matter how many times I told myself not to slip quarters in there, I did anyway. But these jeans molded to me in a loose kind of way, blending in so I forgot they were there. They fit me perfectly, and they were great as long as you didn't look too close.

5 Palm Leaves

The Metrorail rattled above US-1, carrying me south. A trampled McDonald's bag slid back and forth under my feet. The little girl in the next seat was pressed against the window, watching the traffic slide by. She combed her toy pony with such determination, she almost ripped out its mane. I smiled and she smiled back.

My styrofoam cup of café con leche had gone cold. I chewed on the cup, chiseling half-moons in the rim, glanced out the bleary window and watched the strip malls whiz past. They were already decked out for Halloween: black cats and smiling ghosts, witches and scarecrows.

In elementary school, I learned the alphabet and multiplication tables. I learned about legends and mythology. I learned that motion is measured in distance and time.

I did not learn how to make friends. At least, none who stuck around long.

There was Mark Wienman, who taught me dirty words in Latin. Dave Brieske, who believed that the moon landing was fake. The kid down the street, Danny-what's-his-name. We played Quake at his house a couple times before I moved. Danny had a bearded dragon for a pet. He fed it live crickets that he carried in a bag puffed with air. The crickets always escaped. You could hear them chirping in the downstairs den.

My teachers blabbed on and on about building the perfect track record: urging me to take A.P. Spanish, play the trumpet, try out for soccer, whatever looked good on my transcript. Except that I didn't give a shit about college. That's all I needed: more school, stuck in a dorm filled with wall-to-wall idiots, trapped in a place I couldn't leave.

Dad used to march down the hall, storm into my bedroom, and launch into speech after speech about time wasted on the computer.

"It's a nice day. Why are you spending it holed up in here?" he would say, sitting on the edge of my bed, gawking at the posters on the wall: Green Day's heart-shaped grenades.

So I bought a lock for my door.

Dad didn't get it. I sucked at sports, a fact that he was forced to acknowledge no matter where we moved. At one school, everybody worshipped the baseball team, like they were gods with lightning bolts instead of wooden bats. They wore jerseys to class on game days so everybody would look at them and stand in awe of their specialness.

The same thing happened at the next school, and the next. Replace baseball with football or basketball. Same deal. If you could kick a ball or whack it with a stick, everything was cool. This meant two things:

I had no social life.

I was a nonentity.

In ninth grade at Palm Hammock, I met Collin, who rode the bus with me. Collin kept a box of fireworks in his garage, and when he finally learned to drive, we cruised to the boat ramp at night and blew shit up. One time, we brought a bunch of old G.I. Joes. We propped Snake Eyes on a rock, stuffed a firecracker between his legs, and watched him sputter and pop. Collin documented the event with his video camera.

"That's awesome, man. Nice and burnt," he said in this lispy monotone. "Yo. Throw me the lighter."

We dropped the remaining G.I. Joes in an empty Gatorade bottle. Crunched up balls of tinfoil and crammed them in, too. Doused the mess with Works toilet cleaner from the Dollar Store, shook the bottle until it melted and fumed. Then boom. We ran like hell. Collin would fling a Works bomb into the air at the last possible second, while I crouched behind a stump, plugging my fingers in my ears.

Collin wasn't a jock, but he had this weird obsession with ultimate frisbee. As far as I could tell, girls mostly ignored him, although this one skinny senior chick, Ali Brewer, asked him to prom, and he never shut up about it.

I said, "So what? I heard she asked everybody in the whole damn school."

"Yeah, well, the most you've done is…Let's see. Make out with a girl you met on the Internet, thanks to the profile I set up for you."

It was Collin who introduced me to weed. He got it from his brother, who got it from who knows where. We'd smoke up in the parking lot before first period. Collin said it would chill me out. Mr. Future Med Student could ramble on for hours about the molecular structure of marijuana and its effects on the brain.

It's embarrassing to admit this, but I'd been having panic attacks at school. At least, that's how Collin diagnosed me. I'd be sitting at my desk, staring at the back of Kelsey McCormick's head, and then I would die in slow motion. That's what it felt like. My chest would tighten, my lungs would explode as I struggled to inhale-exhale. Everybody was breathing my air. It felt like they were laughing at me, as if my thoughts were broadcast on the TV along with the morning announcements.

It was worse during PE. In the locker room, the jocks would pound me, leaving purple bruises that didn't fade for days. I ducked into a stall when I had to change into my gym clothes. I was so freaked out, I didn't even bother to shower. Just walked around smelling like ass for the rest of the day.

Guess I was having some kind of nervous breakdown. Between the stuff going on at school, my dad basically living in a war zone, and everybody else telling me to figure out my life in the next five minutes, I just couldn't deal with it anymore. I'd talk a teacher into giving me a bathroom pass, then waste time hiding in there. I'd crank all the faucets and listen to the water spurting out just to block the noise inside my head.

After a while, I started smoking during school. I'd sneak off to the parking lot and take a hit during lunch. Then another the minute I got home. It was like I couldn't function without it. Word somehow got out among the low-level smokers that I was the one to see if you needed a few hits for the weekend. I never sold much, just if I had extra from Collin's brother's hookup. Of course, nobody invited me to parties or anything, but some of the girls acted real nice. This one chick, Danica Stone, would stroke my arm during math class. It felt amazing, her long fingers sliding up and down.

Obviously, my social life was a joke. I used to buy these lameass books about magic and sleight-of-hand, hoping my card tricks would impress girls. I never got a chance to find out.

Collin wasn't much help. The farthest he ever drove was the mall. I'd slump in the food court, watching him scarf frozen yogurt while he explained why I should cut my hair. He didn't know the truth. The techno he blasted in his car made me want to vomit. When he dragged me to thrift stores and wedged my bare feet into a pair of broken-down boots, I smelled dead grandfathers in those places and my pulse jumped. Besides, nothing ever fit me.

We used to skate in the park together, until Collin said he was "too old" for it a few years later. Really, he was just lazy. We called ourselves the Two Amigos. He didn't know that I only sat with him at lunch because we had gone through freshman and sophomore years together, riding the bus with those older boys, the ones that slunk around, looking for a way to break you.

When you're little, everyone tells you to "be yourself," as if these words could solve all your problems. They don't tell you the truth: nobody really wants you to be yourself.

"So this thing about you joining the military. It's bogus, right?" Collin asked, as we roamed the aisles at Walmart, our only source of amusement at three in the morning.

My family had been pressuring me to join the armed forces. Go directly to boot camp, do not pass go. Why the hell not? I came from a clan of military men. I had to live up to their standards, even if I secretly doubted that I could ever please them.

I inspected a Snackmaster All-In-One Dehydrator. "Check it out. You can make your own beef jerky."

"Nice way to change the subject," Collin said.

"Maybe I don't feel like talking about this right now." I hid the Snackmaster inside a barbeque grill display, which was decorated with plastic hamburger patties.

"You never talked about it before," Collin said. "Don't

take this the wrong way, but you're not exactly my definition of a hero."

"Gee. Thanks," I said, kicking a shopping cart across the linoleum. "You're not my idea of an Ivy Leaguer."

"Oh snap. Sweet comeback," said Collin, grabbing hold of the cart and pushing it out the door. I followed him into the empty parking lot. Collin was right. I'd always fantasized about busting the bad guys, but that didn't mean I could hack it. Half of my uncles were army guys. It was the default option, according to Collin, who was graduating a year ahead of me. He wouldn't stop bragging about his acceptance letter from Tufts.

He started slicking back his hair. He wore aftershave that reeked like floor cleaner and when I called, he wasn't home. On the rare occasion we hung out, there wasn't much to say.

"Man, I can't wait to get out of here," Collin said, climbing into the cart.

"What? Walmart?"

"This," he said, spreading out his arms. "You want to end up like them?" He jabbed a finger at the trucks crawling along the turnpike.

"I'm just sick of school," I said, giving the cart a shove.

"I hear that," Collin said. "But your grades don't suck. What's the deal?"

"It's not about grades."

School never fazed me. It was the space in between,

the lunchrooms and PE fields, the faces in the hall, that left me numb.

"You better start pumping iron," Collin said.

I pushed the cart a little faster. "Why?"

"Because the army is going to kick your ass."

I smashed my weight into the cart. Collin jumped off just as it tipped and slammed into a creek behind the parking lot. It sat there, half-submerged in muddy water, its wheels spinning around and around.

That was the last time I talked to Collin, my so-called best friend. I tried calling his house. He never called back. His mom said he'd gone shopping for dorm stuff: a coffee maker and a duvet. I juggled the word *duvet* in my brain until it made no sense.

I got off the train at Dadeland South Station and hustled across the busy intersection. The air smelled like car exhaust and the sweet smoke of burning meat, thanks to the BBQ spot nearby. When the light changed, I made a mad dash to the bookstore. A Lexus blared its horn, as if I was committing some crime by crossing the street.

When I walked inside the bookstore, it felt like everybody was watching me, from the white-haired woman checking out the Monet calendars, to the Little League boy in the café practicing his times tables. No sign of Morgan and her Cleopatra hair.

I circled around the entire store, then I finally saw

her at a table, slurping coffee from one of those complicated, dome-shaped cups from Starbucks. She wore a pair of wooden flip-flops and a dress so frilly it swallowed her whole. The buttons below her neck were shaped like butterflies. I spent a lot of time staring at them as walked toward her.

Morgan had a bunch of art magazines spread across the table, along with her sketchbook. Its pages had swollen it to almost twice its natural size. I took out a pen and drew a smiley face on the cover.

"Hey. No vandalizing," she said, smacking me away. "Don't you realize that you're breaking the law?"

"How so?"

"You're BYOCing in a bookstore."

I pulled up a chair. "What the hell are you talking about?"

"Bringing your own coffee."

My fingers curled around the styrofoam cup. "Keep it a secret."

"It's cool. I'm on a first-name basis with the entire staff." As if to prove her point, she waved to the dude at the coffee counter. He was counting change without looking up. "Here's a present for you," she said, slipping a rubber band around my wrist. She held her hand there for a second. "Fits perfectly."

"Thanks," I said, then looked around some more. "What's the story?"

"I worked here last summer. But I got axed."

"For what?

She grinned. "If I told you, I'd have to kill you."

"So it's like that, huh?"

She mashed her hands together and bent forward. "Afraid so," she whispered. "I was stealing books."

"That takes balls. I mean, who robs a freaking bookstore?"

"It wasn't really stealing. I was borrowing," she said, flicking her straw at me.

"Nice. That hit me in the ear," I told her. "By the way . . . this is a store. Not a library. You're supposed to buy things."

Morgan gnawed her straw. "I'm not a big believer in capitalism."

"So what's up with the long dress?" I asked. Not the slickest move in the world. Why couldn't I shut up while I was ahead?

Her neck turned red. She was even cuter when she blushed. "It's freezing in here, right?"

"Not really," I said, confused.

"Don't you love my ensemble?" she blurted out. "It's so *Little House on the Prairie*. I got it at Miami Twice on Bird Road. You should go there sometime."

"Sure," I said. Yeah. I should've just tattooed these words on my forehead: I. Have. No. Game.

"Let's blow this joint," she said, grabbing her bag and scattering the avalanche of magazines on the floor. I noticed a photo on the front cover of *TIME:* an American soldier leaping out of a helicopter, caught between the plane and the desert, stuck, frozen in the moment. I flipped it open and found Dad's name in the credits. My stomach burned, like I was about to start crying or throw up or both, if that's possible.

Dad never let me touch his cameras, which were decorated with strips of masking tape and "A+." I thought this was some kind of positive-thinking trick, like a pep talk. When I asked about it, he said, "No, son. That's my blood type."

The guy behind the counter glared.

"Could you pick that up?" he asked. He wasn't really asking.

"We could," said Morgan. She still didn't move. It was almost funny, but I didn't feel like laughing.

The bookstore dude was pissed. "Now. Pick it up."

"Isn't that your job?"

He stared at her.

"For god's sake." She reached down and plopped the magazines on the table. A bunch of people turned around and shushed us.

"Yo. I'm calling the manager," the guy said, grabbing the phone.

"Whatever," said Morgan.

"Okay, troublemaker," I said. "Let's get out of here."

By this time, my ears were tingling and I couldn't find the door fast enough.

"So you've traveled around a lot?" asked Morgan, as we made our way through the sweltering parking lot.

I got the feeling she was trying to place me in some category and couldn't settle on one yet.

We climbed into her "suburban assault vehicle," a dented Ford Explorer. The bumper was plastered with faded stickers—everything from the Miami Dade Humane Society to Apple computers, along with local bands like Poison the Well and Jacuzzi Boys. If I could've given Morgan a heads-up, I'd tell her to keep her car clean, but I wasn't there to dish out warnings.

I climbed into the passenger seat, scrambling over a heap of crumpled soda cans.

"Sorry about the mess." Morgan cranked the engine and rolled down the windows, just a crack. A blast of heavy bass squirted out of the radio speakers, what my old band teacher would've called a crescendo. "Is this one of those pirate radio stations?" She winced. "They play this song like a hundred times a day."

"You call this a song?" I snorted. "Sounds like the seventh circle of hell."

"Never heard of them. Were they on Total Request Live?" She asked. I couldn't tell if she was joking. She popped the glove box, rustled around inside, pulled out a tiny sandwich bag and something metallic, as slim as a credit card.

"Ever read *The Divine Comedy*?" I asked.

"Nope," she said, sprinkling weed into the circular dent at the end of the card. "Is it funny?"

"Hilarious."

"That would make a great name for my band... if I had a band." Morgan jerked the steering wheel and made an illegal U-turn out of the parking lot. She reached for her tote bag, found a Zippo that said *South Beach* in fancy cursive. When she lit up, the damp vegetable smell of pot hung heavy in the car.

Man, I could've used a hit. This girl was making me nervous. She was on another level I could never hope to reach.

"I'm trying to get a band going," she said before lapsing into a fit of deathlike coughing. "Basically, I had a band. Past tense. It was just Skully playing the piano and me singing. Sort of like Mates of State. Only we sucked."

I nodded like I understood.

"And we were, like, eight years old," she added. "That's why I hang out with Skully. Our checkered pasts."

Morgan smile wickedly and dangled the pipe in front of me. A million thoughts raced through my mind: What if we got pulled over? What if she crashed?

"I'll pass."

"You sure?" She waved it back and forth, as if trying to hypnotize me. "Aren't you the boy who's always drawing pot leaves on your notebook?"

"That's just for show."

Morgan twisted around to look at me. "I know the truth, right?"

"What's that?"

She grinned. "You're really a narc."

The car grew quiet.

I tried to laugh, but the air got caught in my throat. "I just don't smoke when I'm drinking."

"I hear that," she said, laughing.

Morgan shifted and the Explorer stalled in the middle of US-1. Cars honked and swerved around us while she jiggled the stick. "Okay, okay." She gasped. "Give me a second." At last, the engine roared and we lurched forward.

"Hey. What about the Silver Palm Leaves?" I asked.

"You'd christen my band after a smoking accessory?"

"It's the perfect name. Not to mention, the classic design of the nineties."

"I prefer Circle of Hell," said Morgan.

"Hey. Did you hear about the hole they dug in Siberia?"

"Who's 'they'?"

"I don't know. These scientists or something. They dropped a microphone into the hole and they heard people screaming down there, like an entrance to hell."

Morgan fiddled with the radio, clicking past static. She settled on 90.5, "our local college station," The Voice. "Why would they drop a microphone into the hole?"

"No idea. I looked it up online. It doesn't really sound like hell, though," I told her. "More like Dadeland Mall on a Saturday afternoon."

"Now that *is* the seventh circle of hell."

Both of us giggled over this for a while. We could've

talked about the most random shit and that was cool with me. I'd never felt like that before. This was majorly weird because: number one, I could be myself with Morgan. But on the other hand, I wasn't being myself at all. I was nervous and not nervous at the same time. Weird.

She revved the engine, and we punched through a red light. My pulse was beating everywhere, in my throat and fingertips, and although I wasn't driving or smoking, I was the one who felt guilty.

6 The Party House

The party house was the real deal. According to Morgan, some big-shot architect designed it for Skully's rich parents. The triple-decker building overlooked Biscayne Bay. You'd think they wouldn't need a pool, but they had that, too—Olympic-sized, heated, and filled with salt water.

We pulled around the corner, past the DEAD END STREET signs. Headlights speared the palm leaves. A million cars had parked on the grass, long rows of tank-sized SUVs and sharklike convertibles. People scattered into the street, clutching bottles, smoking cigarettes.

"There's Danica Stone," I said, pointing to a girl in a sparkly tube top, remembering her nails on my arm last year.

Morgan made a face. "That skank freaks me out. Why is she here?"

"Everyone is here," I said.

And it was true. Man, I was already starting to shake.

I climbed out and started walking with the crowd.

"It's like trick-or-treating," Morgan said.

"That explains your costume."

"Shut up, Mr. Abercrombie," she said. "This dress is not a costume. It's vintage."

I wanted to tell her that everyone was in costume, whether they knew it or not. Me most of all.

Skully's driveway was paved with gravel. My sneakers crunched as I made my way across it.

"Sounds like somebody eating a bowl of cereal." Morgan laughed and I laughed, too.

"Where's the front door?" I asked.

Up close, the house was even more confusing, like an abstract painting. Or a prison. Only a single row of windows stretches across the middle of the place, up on the second floor.

"At the top of those stairs," she said, pointing toward the other end of the building. "But nobody goes that way."

The steps were hidden by a wall. At the bottom, a skinny strip of concrete extended parallel to the driveway, narrow as a sidewalk. A couple of skaters were taking turns rattling across it and jumping off a plastic milk crate.

Morgan called out to an older dude with a bucket hat and a mustache so long, it curled at the edges. "Hey, Finch. Want me to teach you how to skate?"

"Bite me," he said, not looking.

But when he noticed it was Morgan talking, he collapsed into a grin. She kissed him on the cheek—the standard Miami greeting. I twisted the rubber band tighter around my wrist.

He looked me up and down. "Nice bracelet."

I stopped messing with the rubber band. "Thanks. It was a present."

He laughed as if I'd told an especially funny joke. I just stared at the ground, at the cigarette butts swimming in the gravel.

Morgan kept talking as we filed through the front door. Or was it the back door?

"Finch is like, the only real person here. Except for Skully, of course," she said.

That didn't sound right. I thought Morgan knew a lot of people at Palm Hammock. I was kind of counting on it. Of course, that depended on your definition of "knowing" someone. Her profile online—the Polaroid picture and the poem she had uploaded—showed another side that I'd never seen in class.

"Who is that guy?" I asked. "Does he go to our school?"

"Not in the present tense."

"What?" I was having a hard time, keeping up.

Morgan smirked. "I mean, he graduated."

She didn't bother to explain further.

We pushed through the dancing crowd. I squinted in the semidarkness, wincing at the smell of beer and sweat.

Couples were draped everywhere. There was no way to ignore them.

"Give me some fire," Morgan said, giggling. "Don't lose the Zippo. I can only hold onto it for a few days. Or I just steal my stepmom's."

A group of guys in baseball caps had gathered around a turntable. The music pounded against my chest, more beat than melody. It was too hot in there. I leaned against the wall, closed my eyes, and kept reminding myself to breathe.

"Hey, are you okay?"

Morgan was beaming up at me, her eyes almost level with my chin. She did this cute thing, puffing her lower lip and blowing her bangs aside.

"I'm all right." Actually, I wasn't.

"You don't look all right. I mean, for a second I thought you were going to pass out or something."

"I said I'm all right."

She looked hurt. "Sorry I asked."

I felt like I had to explain. "It's just that I get these ... weird feelings when I'm in a tight space."

"Like claustrophobia? I get that too." She moved closer, pushing a cold bottle in my hand.

Red Stripe. The bottle dripped all over my feet. I took a long gulp. It tasted like lighter fluid.

"Better?" she shouted.

I took another sip, burning a trail down my throat. Morgan kept staring. Her mouth opened and closed.

"You have a lot of hair," she said.

"So do you," I said. "Where's Skully?"

"I think she went to the docks."

"The docks?" I glanced around, as if I could see through the walls. "I didn't know we were so close to the water."

"It's low tide now. Don't you smell it?" Morgan grabbed my hand and yanked me into the living room. She grinned as she tugged me along. "Come on. I'm hiding from my ex."

Couples had scattered into corners, making out in a lazy sort of way. Others were grinding against each other, keeping time with the throbbing bassline. A skinny girl took a drag on her cigarette, blowing smoke between her boyfriend's lips. Nobody had ever invited me to parties like this. Until all this police stuff, I had pushed all the emotions out of my system. Now I was on high frequency, soaking up the newness of things. I couldn't stand the thought of going back and becoming that person again, the loser who hid in the bathroom.

I was taking mental notes, trying to size up everybody. I didn't see any self-proclaimed "druggies," like those sunken-eyed actors in public service announcements. No boys snorting cars and boom boxes up their noses, nobody morphing into snakes. No leather-jacketed dealers getting pounded by Ninja Turtles.

In the living room, a few people I didn't recognize had gathered around a flat screen. A boy who looked a couple years younger than Haylie (I could never tell kids' ages) was messing with a plastic guitar.

"Ever play Guitar Hero?" Morgan asked.

"I suck."

"Me too," she said. "But I kick ass on old-school Atari games like Galaga."

I followed her up a spiral staircase. On the second floor was a kitchen fit for a TV chef. Morgan opened the fridge and rooted around the half-empty shelves. I noticed a tiny bottle in the so-called "crisper."

"What's that?" I asked.

"Sebastian's insulin," Morgan explained. "Skully's little brother."

Her brother? That must've been the kid I saw.

The sink was overflowing with Corona bottles. Beside it was a digital scale, a few crumpled twenties, and a coffee grinder flooded with the chewed-up remains of green leaves. Kryptonite. High-quality stuff. I knew all too well.

"Superman's downfall," said Morgan.

"Looks like we missed out," I said. Obviously, someone was selling it. Not enough to warrant a bust, though, and I didn't have a name. I needed to find who was supplying. In other words, who was the shot caller? The million-dollar question.

I glanced around the kitchen. "Where do they get it?"

"In the garage. Up in the ceiling," she said. Not exactly the answer I wanted. "There's more where that came from. Just like MTV Cribs," she said, helping herself to another beer. "Breakfast of champions. Do you have something to open this with?"

"Sorry."

"No worries." She angled the bottle against the marble countertop and smacked it. The cap skittered across the floor and beer sloshed everywhere. "What can I get you? A hotdog bun? Some mayonnaise?"

"I guess Skully's parents eat out a lot."

"Her mom and dad? They don't even live here," she told me.

"What do you mean?" I asked.

"They live next door."

I must've looked confused because she burst out laughing. "There's a little guest house thing where the nanny used to live—back when they had a nanny. Now they stay there. I mean, when they're in town, which is almost never. And Skully and her brother have this huge place to herself. Except for her *abuela*."

"Her what?"

"Her grandma. She lives in the actual guest house. Takes out her hearing aid whenever Skully throws a party."

Morgan grabbed a lime and crammed it into her bottle, stuffing it down with her thumb. "Once Skully's older brothers moved out, the house got too big. At least, that's what her parents said."

"They must be doctors or lawyers or something."

"Who knows?" she said. "I have no clue what they do. Oh, wait. I lied. On weekends they rent this place."

"Like a hotel?"

"No. Like a location. All these fashion people take pictures for magazines here. You'll see trailers parked out front and all these skinny-ass models prancing around like it's the Playboy mansion or something. I helped out on a shoot once. Got to stand in the boiling sun for hours, holding a bounce card to reflect the light. My arms almost fell off."

I couldn't really imagine it. I mean, my mom could be a major pain in the ass. But who'd want to live all alone this big house?

"Sounds like fun," I said, looking out the window. From there, the driveway almost seemed to glow.

"I'm going to major in art next year. Got my portfolio and everything," she said.

"You're going to do fashion photos and stuff?"

"Hell no. I'm not that superficial."

"What kind of camera do you use?"

"I'm more into drawing than taking pictures. I know. When someone says 'art' these days, you automatically think 'photography.'"

"I didn't say that."

"You were thinking it. Get this. I don't even own a camera. I just borrow my ex-boyfriend's," she said. "Have you picked a major yet?"

"What are you? My mom?"

Morgan flushed. "Sorry. I didn't mean to get up in your business."

"It's okay." Jeez. No wonder I was a social retard. I

couldn't even have a conversation with a girl without pissing her off. Only one thing to do now.

"Hey. Do you have any change?" I asked.

She gave me a funny look. "I'm not a vending machine."

"You sure?" I said, pulling a nickel from her ear.

"Oh, my god. My perverted uncle used to get drunk and do shit like that," she said. "Can you make it disappear?"

I put the nickel on the counter. Pressing down with my palm, I hid the coin between my knuckles, faking surprise when I flipped my hand over.

She giggled. "Are you going to pull it out of my ear again?"

"I'm not that good."

"You're magic. Don't deny it."

This was totally untrue. Right at that moment, I felt like an asshole.

Morgan gulped the last of her Corona and plopped the bottle in the sink.

"To the boat docks," she said.

7 Crossfade

The docks were crammed with people when we reached them. Some of them sat swinging their legs on a concrete seawall by the water. Others wandered around, clutching plastic cups and flashlights. Music thumped from a turntable, propped on a stack of cement blocks.

I saw Skully hoist herself onto the seawall and stand there, wobbling on her heels. For a second, I thought she might fall, but she managed to find her balance. I couldn't get over her Frankenstein boots and weird tank top. Not to mention her reverse mullet. Morgan's dresses were one thing, but Skully was something else. It took guts to wear whatever the hell you wanted. Or maybe she didn't give a shit.

A couple of girls walked past her, laughing. "Jump," one of them called out. I got the feeling that they didn't

69

know Skully at all. I doubted that half the people at this party knew her real name.

"Are we having fun yet?" Skully spun around in a circle and for the first time, I noticed the tattoos on her back: a pair of feathery wings. Her stare cut across the crowd like a searchlight. I walked closer.

"I really like your house," I told her.

She rolled her eyes. "Did Morgan give you the grand tour?"

"I tried," she said.

"I bet you did." Skully took a gulp from her plastic cup and giggled, spilling liquid down her chin.

"Skully acts wasted all the time, but she's almost straight-edge," said Morgan.

"Almost," Skully added. "Except for these." She dangled her pack of cloves. "I'm allowed one vice."

So my supposed alpha dog was straight-edge. This wasn't what I expected. I wasted my time, coming here. Another false start. Skully was so desperate for friends, she just let everybody party at her fancy house and do whatever the hell they wanted.

But if Skully wasn't supplying, then who was my next target? I peered up at the seawall, but she had disappeared. I pictured the wings on her back unfolding gently, like a fan, and lifting her into the sky.

"Didn't you say that Skully could hook me up?" I asked Morgan.

She shrugged. "Not her personally. I meant you could get some at her party."

"Who then?" I was starting to sound desperate.

Morgan wasn't listening. She waved her hands to the music, lost in her own world. As we made our way toward the water, she beamed a flashlight at me. I squinted in a flood of brightness, stepping into a place so unfamiliar, I might've walked onto the moon.

"What's stressing you?" she asked.

"Nothing. Everything."

"That's all?" she said, pulling closer. "Let's see. Nobody knows you well enough to hate you."

"What's that supposed to mean?"

"People in this school can be kind of fake," she said.

For a moment, we just stood there, soaking up the silence. I was with Morgan Baskin and I didn't know what to do: whether to get up and leave or lean closer. I kept thinking what it would be like to kiss her. My thoughts rushed with the things I'd seen online: her poem, the Polaroid of her scars. What else was there that I couldn't see?

Morgan dipped her head toward mine, moving so close, her eyelashes tickled. "Can you do magic again?"

She took my face in her hands and we tilted into a kiss. I was breaking all kinds of rules right then, but instead of pulling away, I slid my tongue around her mouth. Now I was aware of too many things: the smell of her shampoo, the Red Stripe I downed earlier, and voices in the distance, like the buoys tolling across the bay.

We kissed under the Big Dipper, the only heavenly object I knew by name. Long ago, the Greeks looked up, noticed scorpions and centaurs. All I could see was a lopsided spoon.

"Hey, Morgan."

Skully stood a few feet away, her shirt snapping in the breeze.

"What are you guys doing out here?" she asked.

Morgan smoothed the sand off her jeans. "Looking for you," she lied.

"I'm not hard to find," Skully said, narrowing her eyes. If she'd seen the kiss, she didn't let on.

God. That kiss. What the hell was I thinking? I wasn't thinking. Not with my head, anyway. It's not like I'd had many chances to make out with a hot girl. *Carpe diem*, as Collin used to say. From here on out, I had to be more careful.

We followed Skully around the house, and Morgan drifted away. Clumps of skinny kids sat on plastic chairs facing the water. I watched a girl on a guy's lap, taking pictures with her iPhone. This party was a false lead. Maybe I needed to find a different crowd before it was too late to blend anywhere.

Skully scooted next to me. "Having fun?"

"Not really."

"Morgan can be so boring at parties," Skully told me. "She's too busy building up her clientele."

"What do you mean?"

She smirked. "You're joking, right?"

I watched Morgan weave her way through the chairs. She was talking to one of the skaters I bumped into earlier.

He dangled a baggie. "So where's the rest of it?"

"Don't try to act like I gave you a slack bag."

Their voices grew louder, but I couldn't hear them clearly anymore. "Let's talk," was the last thing I heard her say, as she and her customer slunk behind the house. I took a step, but Skully held me back.

"Chill," she said. "Morgan can handle herself."

"So she's a dealer," I said. Not Skully. The girl in the vintage dress with the butterfly buttons was my alpha dog?

"Bingo, detective." Skully giggled. "But I wouldn't use the word *dealer*. Morgan is more of an entrepreneur, though she hasn't quite mastered the art of finance. For instance, she blows all the good shit on her friends and doesn't charge them a dime."

"I thought you didn't smoke."

Skully shrugged. "What can I say? In junior high, I used to hang out in the parking lot with all the stoners because I liked talking to them. They didn't diss me for not joining in."

"Where is she getting it from?"

"What is this? Twenty questions?" She looked over her shoulder. "Check out Spiderman over there."

On the boat docks, I caught a glimpse of Brent grabbing onto those heavy chains that lower yachts into the bay.

I watched him swing over the water like a caped crusader. His spiky hair rippled like feathers. A few people clapped.

"If he falls, I'm not fishing him out," said Skully.

I was so over this party. My head was pounding. How could Morgan be the one I was after? She was this cute girl in my history class, an ex-ballerina who drew her own comics. Where the hell was she now? And with who? I had to call her and get this figured out. I reached into my pocket.

My phone wasn't there.

Shit.

This was bad. Really bad. If anyone found my cell and the numbers in it, I could lose everything. I tried to keep calm. I wasn't supposed to call my contact unless it was an emergency. The number wasn't identified on the phone, only the name Carlos. Still, I'd messed up. Big time.

"Has anyone seen my phone?" I called out, receiving only blank stares in response.

A crackle erupted from the backyard. Then a hiss. Then a musical series of pops.

Skully pointed at the roof. "They're setting off bottle rockets. What a bunch of idiots. Come on. Time to jet before the *policia* arrive," she said, tugging my arm.

"Where's Morgan?" I asked. A dozen scenarios flashed through my brain: Morgan on the ground, the deal gone wrong, blood in the grass.

Everyone scattered. As we tore around the front of Skully's house, a rectangle of light sliced the gravel. Across the street, a woman stood in her doorway, hunched in a bathrobe.

"It's four in the bloody morning," she said, like an actress on *Dr. Who*.

"Only you can prevent forest fires," Skully yelled.

The woman waved a flashlight at us. "I'm calling the police."

Skully ran through the backyard. I stumbled in the grass and tried to catch my breath. The Roman candles kept sizzling, beads of colored flame swooping across the pines as if someone had lit them all at once. I remembered buying fireworks with Collin, how we laughed at the warning on the box: *Light Fuse and Get Away!!!!*

When I reached the car, there was no sign of Morgan.

"Stay here," Skully said, as if talking to a dog. Then she bolted toward the trees.

I leaned against the bumper, watching everyone flood past: the party girls half-jogging with their shoes flung over their shoulders, the boys tossing bottles into the street. Okay. This sucked beyond all recognition. There was the sound of glass tinkling, then a jolt of pain surging up my arm. I looked down at the ribbons of blood slashed into my skin. The more I stared, the harder it stung.

"Looks like you got in a ninja fight with a cactus," said Morgan, sneaking up beside me, "and the cactus won."

"Skully was trying to find you," I explained. "These idiots were throwing bottles all over the place. And I lost my cell phone."

"I know," she said, handing it over.

A wave of sickness washed over me. Whether I liked it or not, Morgan was my suspect now. She was the last person I'd want to find messing with my phone. I flipped it open. All the numbers were there, blinking back at me.

Morgan said, "I wouldn't go dropping it in people's driveways."

"Is that where you found it?" I asked.

"Buried in the gravel."

"It must've fallen out of my pocket." Still, that didn't make any sense.

She peeled off her cardigan and dabbed my arm. "Can't have you bleeding on my fake leather upholstery. Good thing I paid attention in Girl Scouts."

Did Morgan pick my pocket? I couldn't shake the feeling that she was playing me.

"Thanks," I muttered.

Cars squealed down the road, their headlights so bright they seemed solid. The lights merged into spinning discs, blue and red, and I knew that the neighbor wasn't kidding about calling the cops.

"Get in the car," Morgan said, her smile gone. "You're driving."

"I am?"

I slid into the driver's seat. "What about Skully?"

No answer.

I revved the engine. We rolled backward into the neighbor's driveway. I jerked the wheel and we spun around as Morgan directed me to.

"I thought this was a dead-end street," I said, as we careened over potholes.

"We're taking a shortcut," she said.

The Explorer rattled across a fallen tree limb. I clenched my teeth as the tires bounced over twigs and rocks. In the darkness, it was hard to see. Branches flailed and scraped against the window. I twisted around in my seat, caught the lights flaring in the distance.

We pulled up beside a chain link fence. A section had toppled into the ground, all twisted.

"Where the hell are we going?" I asked, rubbing my sore arm.

"Take a guess," Morgan said.

The car launched forward with a jolt as I drove over the mangled fence and swerved into a swampy thicket of oak trees. A dirt road curved into some kind of nature preserve, tucked behind Skully's neighborhood. I half-expected a T-Rex to raise its head above the bushes. After circling for a few minutes and finding only dead ends, I let Morgan have it.

"We can't just drive around all night. This is stupid."

She wouldn't even look at me. Her jaw clenched.

We slammed through a field of tall grass. There was the bay, dark as asphalt.

"Stop here," she said.

I coasted closer to the shore and cut the ignition. For some reason, Morgan got out and started walking. I followed.

The ground sparkled with broken glass. Poles jutted from the water. There was a dilapidated old fishing dock, the edges frosted with barnacles. It smelled like mud and salt.

Morgan plunked down on a craggy rock. "This is an old chimney," she explained, as I moved beside her. "A hermit built a house here. Then a hurricane laid waste to the coast. This is all that's left of his humble abode."

"Which hurricane?" I asked.

She shrugged. "Back then, they didn't have names."

We sat on the slab of coral, our feet dangling above the foamy tide. I was staring at the ground, at the plastic six-pack rings and rusty soda cans, the bleach caps and Bic pens. Even a naked Barbie doll buried in the sludge, her hair splayed out like seaweed.

Morgan's fingers slid inside my T-shirt, digging their way across my ribs. "Aaron," she murmured. "Aaron," she said again. "Aaron." She breathed against my neck.

I gently moved her hands away.

"What's the matter?" she asked.

"Nothing. It's just that ... I'm not into this right now."

Another lie.

Without a word, Morgan jumped up and walked toward the car. For a second, I thought she was going to take off without me. She was still sulking when I got in. Morgan cranked the engine, and it stalled with a jerk.

"God damn it," she said, slapping the dash so hard, the

glove box door popped open. Inside was a Ziploc stuffed with weed and beside it, a few rubber-banded stacks of cash. We didn't say anything for a moment.

"Morgan, why are you doing this?" I asked.

"Doing what?"

"You know what."

She still wouldn't look at me. "Why do you care?"

"It's not like you're hurting for money. I want to know why."

"Why not? It's fun."

"Fun? Don't you realize you could go to jail?"

Now I was starting to talk like a cop. If I wasn't careful, I could lose everything.

"Nobody's going to throw me in jail," she said. "I'm not even eighteen. The worst I could do is juvie. But you're forgetting one very important thing."

"What's that?"

She looked at me now. "I'd have to get caught."

———

We cruised down the unpaved street. My teeth clattered with every bump. Soon we were meandering past bright windows and circular driveways. Back to civilization. On the horizon, a power plant gushed mounds of smoke, pale against the night sky, thick as shaving foam.

Morgan drove in silence. I cracked my window, just to fill the space between us.

"Where do you live?" she asked in a monotone, after what seemed like forever.

I was hoping to crash at Skully's place and find a way home in the morning. Now I was stuck. I couldn't think of anything else to say except the truth. "Downtown."

"That's like, an hour away. I'm not schlepping over there."

"I didn't ask you to."

"Fine. Just sit there and don't talk to me."

"There's nothing you want to talk about?"

"Not really," she said, fixing her gaze on the road.

We crossed US-1, which hummed with traffic, even at this hour of the night, past the Taco Bell where kids parked and drank from paper bags until the cops kicked them out. I kept thinking about Skully, wondering if she was okay. I closed my eyes and saw her teetering on the seawall, the wings tattooed into her skin.

"We should call Skully. Make sure she's alive," I said.

"I texted her already," Morgan snapped. That was the end of it.

We pulled up to a gate. It jerked aside with a wobble and we drove through it, past one sprawling house after another, with fountains gurgling on the front lawns, and fences spiked like medieval drawbridges.

Morgan grabbed a remote control from her sun visor, punched a button. Another gate slid away. The driveway was packed with fancy cars. There was no room for the Explorer, so we parked on the lawn.

I got out first and stood next to the car. The sign on the gate said *Bad Dog*, with a picture of a snarling Doberman. A baby swing dangled from a mango tree. Newspapers wrapped in yellow plastic dotted the yard. Morgan reached the front door and turned around.

"You going to stay there all night?" she asked.

Not exactly an invitation.

She unlocked the door. Light flooded the grass and I stood, spotlit, unable to budge.

After a moment, she shook her head and said, "Come on, Aaron. The mosquitoes are nasty. You'll catch West Nile and it will be my fault."

When I stepped inside the house, it felt empty, as if everyone else had disappeared. Morgan ducked into the hallway. She came back with an armful of blankets and dumped them on a couch in the living room. At her heels, a small white dog yipped and sneezed.

"My stepmom's attack poodle," Morgan explained. "She has allergies."

"Your stepmom or the poodle?"

"Both," she said, reaching down to scratch the poodle's ears. "She's like, my ideal dog. But if you ignore her, she'll pee on your bed. Come on," she said and I followed her down the hall. At first, I thought I was sleeping on the couch, but she led me into a bedroom.

Morgan clicked on the light. "You can crash here. Sorry about the mess."

I stepped over an avalanche of clothes heaped on the

floor. On the dresser leaned a castle made of Legos and a baseball cap that said "StarStyled" with a dancer leaping over the word. A mobile threw geometric shadows across the room, making me feel as if I'd sunk underwater.

Looking around Morgan's bedroom didn't lend any clues to what she was really like. In fact, I didn't know this girl any more than she knew me.

She yanked back the bedspread, which was decorated with twirling ballerinas.

"You're really into dance, huh?" I said.

"Isn't every little girl?"

"You're not little anymore."

She frowned. "I was supposed to go to this big deal school for ballet. Obviously, I didn't get in."

"What happened?" I asked.

"Look at me."

"I am looking."

In fact, I was looking all the time.

Morgan shook her head. "You're not getting it. Even when my stepmom put me on a diet..."

"A diet? How old were you?"

"Like, twelve."

"Shit. That's so wrong."

"I know. But I still didn't make the weight requirement. In other words, I'm too fat."

"That's totally not true."

"Yeah, well. Tell that to the dance director."

A pair of tangled headphones toppled on the floor. She scooped it up. "Helps me fall asleep."

"Me too," I said. "You ever dream about music? That's like, the best."

"Doesn't happen to me. At least, I don't think so. I never remember my dreams."

"How can you not remember them?"

"Maybe I don't have any," she said, glancing away.

"Oh, come on. Even my dog has dreams. You see his little feet going . . . " I flapped my fingers in front of her face.

Morgan tossed a pillow at me. She noticed the rubber band around my wrist and tugged it, snapping it against my skin. "You look like shit, by the way," she said. Then she left me there, clutching the pillow in both arms.

I shut the door. At one time, it might've had a lock, but now there was just a splintery hole gaping beneath the doorknob. On the back of the door was a bulletin board rippling with pictures and cards: *BFF, best friends forever. 2 Good 2 B 4-Gotten. Stay sweet! Don't change!*

If only it were that easy.

Everybody changed, whether we wanted to or not.

I couldn't look at this stuff anymore. Just snooping through the cards was enough to drown me in a megadose of guilt. What the hell was I doing? I didn't want to hurt these girls, but that's exactly what I was supposed to do. And I was scared shitless about what was going to happen, but I couldn't decide if I was doing the right thing or not. It was getting harder to tell the difference.

I flipped the light switch and stumbled toward the bed, tripping over things in the dark. I crawled under the covers and gawked at the ceiling, where glow-in-the-dark stars looped and swirled and finally faded away.

8 House of Women

The next morning, I woke up and saw a lady standing in the middle of the bedroom, stuffing clothes into a laundry basket. The lady, with her squat legs and frizzy braid, looked nothing like Morgan.

I hunched down under the covers.

"Hi," I said. What else was I supposed to do?

It was ten o'clock in the morning and she'd already painted herself up: mascara, blush, the whole works. She wore a tank top decorated with rhinestone flamingoes and a pair of sweatpants draped low on the waist.

"I wondered why Morgan was sleeping on the couch. I'm her stepmother, Sheryl," she said, shaking my hand. Her grip was flimsy and dry, like chopsticks. "You go to Palm Hammock?"

"Yes, ma'am."

"And your name?"

"Aaron Foster."

I guess she was one of those "cool stepmoms" who put up with coed slumber parties.

"From whereabouts?" she asked.

"Homestead. We've traveled around a lot."

"Military?"

"Yeah. My dad was in the Air Force."

Her face changed. "Is he ... um ... in active service now? I mean, is he over there?" she asked. "Over there" was what people called the Middle East.

"He's dead," I told her.

This was really awkward. I hated the way she was looking at me, the pity on her face. So I did something dumb. I started blabbering.

"He was in Iran, taking pictures. He said it's different now. They even have a Starbucks. Except it's called Star Box."

"Well," she said. "That's progress."

"Is it?"

The silence swelled around us. Finally, she said, "I am not in favor of this war. But I want you to know that I support our troops."

"My dad wasn't a soldier," I explained, but she was already shuffling down the hall.

I rolled off the mattress and found my shirt wadded under the dresser. My jeans reeked like hell, but I couldn't go walking around in my boxers. In the back pocket, I found my cell. There was a voicemail from my "friend." Great.

"I received a phone call around two-thirty in the morning," the cop said. "No message. Just a lot of background noise. Can you verify this?"

He sounded agitated. Not a good sign. I wasn't supposed to call unless there was a real emergency. Our weekly meetings off-site were our only source of contact.

I called back and made up a lie about leaving the phone in my pocket, how it must've gone off by itself. Pretty lame, I know.

"Don't let it happen again," he said.

"It won't," I said before hanging up.

The Narcotics team wasn't the only one looking for me. Haylie must've sent a million text messages. By now, Mom was probably coming home from her shift at the hospital. The student nurses always got stuck with the worst "rotations." I didn't think about it much, but Mom's version of school was crappier than mine.

I texted Haylie our little secret message: OLA KALA. In Greek, it means, "everything's okay." That's what Dad used to tell us.

Haylie: Are you dead?

Me: Not yet.

Haylie: Liar.

Me: Slept at friend's house.

Haylie: GIRL friend?

Me: Something like that.

Haylie: !!!!!

Me: Cover for me. Please?

Haylie: OK. But what do I get?

Me: Driving lessons.

Haylie: Deal.

In the sun-drenched kitchen, the smell of pancakes hit me. My stomach tightened. I could see my reflection in every gleaming appliance, from the stainless-steel fridge to the stove, which looked brand-new, as if nobody had ever used it.

Sheryl pulled out a chair. "Sit."

I plunked myself down at the table. For some reason, I couldn't stop scratching my ankles. When I peeled back my sock, the skin looked bumpy and swollen.

"Are the mosquitoes biting?" Sheryl asked.

"I don't know. I've got this weird rash."

She checked it out. "You must be allergic to mangoes."

"What?"

"The trees in the front yard. I've been begging Dave to cut them down. The leaves give me a rash if I touch them. Did you know that mangoes are related to poison ivy?"

She peeked inside the oven, which was crammed with Tupperware. "I was going to make bacon but I can't find the frying pan," she said, looking a little flushed. She opened the microwave and thrust a plate in front of me.

"Butter or syrup?" she asked.

"Yes, please."

She laughed.

My mom wasn't big on anything "instant," which included pancakes that came ready-made in little plastic pouches. They were rock-cold on one side and scalded on the other, but I grabbed a fork and dug in.

Sheryl sat down across from me. "You live where?"

"Downtown," I said between mouthfuls.

"That's a long way to drive."

"My mom didn't like the schools in our area."

She nodded. "Morgan wanted to switch last year. She had such a hard time. Teenage girls can be brutal."

"Sheryl. Oh, my god," said Morgan, strolling into the kitchen with a towel wrapped around her head. "Please stop. Now."

"Fix yourself up," said her stepmom. "I'm talking to … what did you say your name was?"

"Aaron."

"Would you two like to explain something to me?" her stepmom asked.

Morgan looked at the floor. "What's that?"

"The car," said Sheryl.

"What about the car?" said Morgan, still avoiding her stepmom's glance.

"It's scratched, young lady. And guess who's going to pay for the repair?"

Morgan shrugged. "Dad will fix it when he gets back."

"This is your responsibility."

"How do you know it's my fault?" she said, almost shrieking.

"It was me," I said.

They both stared.

"I was the one driving. It's my fault. I'll pay for it. I promise."

Sheryl glared at Morgan. "You let this boy drive your father's car?"

Oops.

"Come here," her stepmom said. "Let's have a little chat, shall we?"

I'd heard that one before.

Morgan and her stepmom headed outside. The front door slammed and my glass of orange juice trembled. Behind the door, I caught Sheryl's voice rising.

"You don't even know this boy," she said.

"He's just a friend," Morgan shot back.

Ouch. The f-word. God. Is that how she saw me?

"He's hiding something," her stepmom hissed. "He said his father was in Iran. Didn't he mean Iraq?"

My dad was taking pictures, not fighting a war. That was his job—observe from a distance. Why was that so hard to understand? I should've made up a lie. Then maybe she'd believe me.

Morgan's voice cut in. "Give him a break, Sheryl."

"That boy just tried to sell me a string of lies."

Could people see through me that easily? I was starting to freak now.

"How long have you known him?" Sheryl went on.

"God. I feel like I'm on trial or something. He goes to my school, okay? We never really talked before. I don't know why."

I'm human wallpaper. And I'm not on your social level. That's why.

"This is your senior year," Sheryl said. "Not the time to be making bad decisions."

"Decisions? You mean I actually get a choice? I thought my life was already decided for me. Community college. And, if I'm lucky, a job selling life insurance or whatever."

"Honey, I know you had your heart set on art school. But I really don't see how drawing pretty pictures is going to get you anywhere."

"Yeah. Like dance was a logical career option."

"You used to love your ballet studio."

"Actually, I hated it. Don't you remember? I begged you to take me out of those classes, and you kept making me do it, year after year. Even when I got sick … "

"Let's not talk about it. You're healthy now. That's all that matters."

This didn't sound like the usual school drama. More like family stuff. God. My mom got on my nerves sometimes, but she was the total opposite of Morgan's freaky stepmother. I couldn't believe what I was hearing.

Sheryl came back with Morgan and said, "Let's get your friend home. Where did you say you lived?"

"I didn't."

"Downtown. Isn't that what you said?"

I didn't want Morgan to know that I lived in a shitty apartment in Wynwood. It was too embarrassing.

"You can just drop me off at the Metrorail."

"Actually, I was going to swing by Lincoln Road," said Sheryl, "so it's really not a problem, stopping downtown. No trouble at all." She flashed her teeth at me.

I winced and smiled back. "Can I have another plate first?"

———

I shouldn't have wolfed down that second helping. My stomach burned like venom as we barreled down the expressway. I sat up front with Sheryl, who knew the words to every hit on the Top 40 countdown and sang along. Loudly. I rubbed my thumb, like Haylie mentioned, but I couldn't shake the stabbing behind my eyes.

"So what's it like, growing up on a military base?" Sheryl asked me.

"Pretty much the same, everywhere you go."

Morgan said, "I thought you lived in another country? That's what you told me, right?"

Yeah, that's what I told her. I'd totally forgotten about that stupid lie. Now I was backpedaling. Again.

"I don't remember much about it. I mean, I was too little," I stammered. "It was kind of a long time ago."

Rain needled down the windshield. Soon we were plowing through a downpour.

"Where now?" asked Sheryl.

"Stay on ninety-five north," I said.

Skyscrapers gleamed along the horizon. I watched the above-ground train, the Metromover, snake over the Miami River.

Sheryl swerved into the exit lane. "Turn off here, right?"

"Not yet," I said.

A car let out a long, lingering honk.

"What the hell, Sheryl?" said Morgan.

"Watch your mouth, young lady." Sheryl flipped off the driver behind them, inciting another round of honks.

We rolled past South Miami Avenue, the tail end of Little Havana, otherwise known as Calle Ocho: boxy apartments with Xed-out windows, as if masking tape could hold against a hurricane.

"Aaron," said Sheryl. "Keep me honest. Are we going the right way?"

"Yes, ma'am," I said, slipping a finger inside my sock.

She hit the gas and we rattled over the potholes. At the end of the block, cars streamed around Burger King. A poster of a cartoon dog said *Perro Perdido* in bold-faced Spanish.

"This is a long way to commute," she said.

"A long way," Morgan agreed.

We inched through a traffic jam at the Brickell Bridge, which had split open to let a tugboat pass beneath it. Rain sprayed off the statue at the base—some dead guy pointing a bow and arrow.

"Look at all this construction," said Sheryl, as if she'd never driven here before. Maybe she hadn't.

By the time we reached my shitty neighborhood, Sheryl had locked the doors and windows. Biscayne Boulevard didn't look any safer in the daylight.

"Check out that crappy building. The paint is flaking like a sunburn," said Morgan, pointing at my apartment.

"It's not that crappy," I said.

As we braked at the intersection, a bum with a Tommy Hilfiger umbrella stumbled into traffic. Two trucks and an SUV swerved around him, blaring their horns, but he just punched his fists at them. I felt bad for the guy. Everybody ignored him, like he was invisible or something. I knew exactly what that was like.

"Turn," I told Sheryl.

"Now?" she said, blinking.

"Make a left."

The bum stalked toward my window and thrust a bouquet of palm fronds at me. Their tips had been braided into weird shapes: grasshoppers and rosebuds. I shook my head. He lurched to the other side of the car.

"No, no." Sheryl hit the wipers. The bum yelped and wobbled backward, clutching his thumb. He burned his gaze into mine, a look of pure rage.

"Shit," I said.

In one quick motion, he grabbed the wiper blade and tugged.

Sheryl slammed her fist on the horn. "Get away from my car."

The wiper snapped like a turkey bone. The bum just stood there, gawking at it. Then he chucked it into the street.

The light still hadn't turned, but Sheryl pumped the gas and we squealed around the corner.

"There's a cop behind us," said Morgan.

"I see him," said Sheryl.

We passed a string of pawnshops, Big Daddy's Bail Bonds, and an abandoned car wash. When we bumped across the train tracks, I looked for a house that might qualify as "family friendly." I only saw wooden shacks, doomed for the bulldozer.

"Are we coming up on your place?" asked Sheryl.

I pinned my gaze to the window. "Yeah. Almost."

The houses were choked by fences and barbed wire. That wasn't going to help. Despite the smell of desperation—sofas rotting on the front porch, laundry flapping in the rain—satellite dishes were bolted to every roof.

I spotted a house with a chain link gate, swung open. No cars out front.

"There," I said.

Sheryl pulled up to the sidewalk and parked. "Honey, can you pass Aaron an umbrella from the backseat?"

Morgan handed me an umbrella with a duck's head on the handle. I got out and fumbled with the lever. When

I finally popped it open, I was already soaked. Morgan got out, too. There was a diaper in the road, smothered in something that resembled hay. I kicked it to the side.

"That's so freaking gross," Morgan said, scooting next to me. "I'm going to throw up."

"The neighbor's dog messes with our garbage," I said as we walked toward the door. Was she going to follow me the entire way?

"Whose baby?" she asked.

"What?" I caught the glow of a television blinking in the window. Either they left the TV on or somebody was home. "Oh, the diaper? I don't know where it came from. Next door, probably."

We looked at each other.

Morgan said, "Aren't you going inside?"

"My mom's probably freaking out. It's going to be ugly," I told her.

"Okay," she said. At that moment, I thought she was onto me, but she turned and marched back to the car, leaving me in the drizzle. I watched her hop into the front seat. The car still didn't leave. I waved. Sheryl cracked the window and wiggled her fingers at me.

I ducked around the side of the house, praying nobody saw me standing on the doorstep like one of those freaky Bible salesmen, the dudes in the dark suits who used to pedal through my neighborhood, two by two, on bikes.

The yard was a wreck. A deflated kiddy pool was crumpled in the weeds, along with a plastic slide. Next door, a dog yapped behind a plywood fence, setting off yips and howls across the block.

Something pressed into the back of my leg. I spun around. A small boy stood in the rain, clutching a toy gun. He pointed it at me.

"What have you got there?" I said, reaching for it.

The kid took aim, making shoot 'em up noises with his mouth. I tried to scoot past him, but he wouldn't move. I smacked his hand and the gun soared into the grass. As the kid bounded after it, I took off running.

I cut through the neighbor's yard, ducking under a clothesline. A pregnant woman was pacing in the driveway. She was talking rapid-fire into a cell phone, holding a dinky umbrella over her head. How stupid was this? I was running like a god damned fugitive in an episode of *Cops*.

I kept sprinting. As I ran, I got a glimpse of other people's Sunday afternoons: the smell of laundry detergent, smoky meat roasting on the grill, portable radios pumping out salsa and reggaeton.

When I got to the Shell station on the corner, the rain had stopped. I crossed the street and followed the gleaming train tracks near the apartment. The rails glinted silver in the sunlight. I hunched down and pressed my ear against warm steel, listening for wheels that had already come and gone.

9 Sweet

The next day, after driving through what felt like miles of swampland, I found the abandoned missile site near Krome Detention Center, on the edge of civilization. A concrete guard shack jutted above the sawgrass. I parked behind it, got out, and crunched through mounds of paintball shells the color of melted crayons.

The cop was waiting near the trenches. Guess that's where they used to launch rockets. Who knew?

"Let's head inside," he said.

I didn't want to go in there, but I followed him down a hallway that reeked of piss. The empty room was studded with exhaust vents. Sunlight squeezed through the holes like windows on a ship.

I opened my mouth and the words tumbled out.

I told him about Skully. "She's basically living by herself at this point. Her parents don't even live in the same house, so it's the perfect place to party. Besides, she's desperate for friends, so all kinds of people just hang out there."

"Did you witness any drug transactions in the house?" the cop asked.

I stared at the razor cuts on his head. "Not really."

"What do you mean, 'not really'?"

I thought about Morgan, all the cards and pictures on her bulletin board. I couldn't do this to her. I just couldn't. So I said, "There was some stuff in the kitchen."

"Stuff? Could you be a little more specific?"

He was losing patience with me. I took another breath. "There was a scale."

"A scale?"

"You know. Like for measuring."

"What else?"

"Well, obviously there was weed there."

"Enough to justify a search warrant?"

"Maybe. I don't know."

The cop got up in my space. He was spitting all over me. "What exactly did you see?"

"It was a party, okay? People were smoking. That's all I saw."

He wasn't buying it. "That's all?"

In the distance, I heard the pow-pow-pow of paintball ammo. I wanted to bust out of there and join the players in the fields, fighting wars where nobody wins or loses. At the end of the day, everyone just gives up and goes home.

The cop leaned closer. "Listen to me and listen good. You need to get close to these kids, reel them in and earn their trust. Understand?"

"Yes, sir."

"Any idea who's the shot caller?" he asked.

I shrugged.

"So you're at this party and you talk to nobody... not a single person..." He trailed off. "What were you doing? Hiding in the bathroom?"

It stung, that little comment. I fell right into his trap. "This girl, Morgan. She was selling."

"Okay. What exactly did you see?"

He waited for me to continue. When I kept quiet, he said, "I don't need to remind you how much your cooperation means. We must help each other."

I help you. You help me.

The cop scratched his chin. "You're protecting her, aren't you?"

True. I was trying to protect everyone: The girls. My family. My own sorry ass.

A slow smile crept across his face. "Okay. Let's cut the bullshit. Protecting her isn't going to do you any good."

I was in so deep, there was no way out. I knew it sounded crazy, but I wondered if there was a way to locate the shot caller without getting the girls in trouble.

"It doesn't make any sense," I said. "Her family is loaded. I don't get why she's doing this."

"I've seen it before," the cop said, folding his hands behind his neck. "She's attracted to the lifestyle. It's exciting for these spoiled rich kids to go slumming in neighborhoods like Wynwood. Makes them feel tough when they dirty up. This is a classic case. Broken home, too much free time, disposable income."

"Morgan is a sweet girl," I said, a little too quickly.

"Aren't they all?" he said and I wanted to push my fist through his teeth.

He didn't know them. He didn't know that Morgan was a cutter, that she carried a jagged piece of metal in her sock. I left out the parts that I kept close to myself: Skully leaning over the seawall, the winged tattoo on her back. Morgan gliding against traffic on her bike, speeding in the wrong direction. Kissing her on the dock, the battered remains of an old hermit's house, ripped apart by a hurricane with no name.

"Look. Don't be getting *too* chummy with these kids."

"What's going to happen to them?" I asked.

He rubbed his forehead. "We need to find out who is supplying. If the girls lead us to the head honcho, they're all going down together. Who knows? In a few weeks, we might be closing in on a bust. That is, if you do your job right. Is that clear?"

Right. What could be right about this? Basically, I was screwed. I kept telling myself that I was doing the right thing, whatever that meant, but I didn't feel right about this. Not at all.

I nodded. "Yes, sir."

10 True Gentleman

On Monday, I drifted through the lunchroom, a social minefield divided by haircuts and sneaker brands. Above the cash register, a sign said *DO NOT THROW FOOD*. In the upper right corner, a fry dangled like a fishing lure.

Across the street, a few people had wandered over to the gas station. They popped into the convenience store and came out with Cokes and microwaved burritos. Some of them sat Indian-style, smack in the middle of the parking spaces.

I waited for the light to change at the intersection. The sun beat down, radiating heat off the sidewalk. When I reached the gas station, I waved to Skully. Unfortunately, she was there with Brent.

"What's shaking?" she asked, clomping in her stupid Frankenstein boots.

"Look," I said. "I'm sorry we ditched your party."

"No worries." Skully offered me a Dorito. I shook my head. She shrugged, then stuffed the entire chip into her mouth. "That party was wack," she said between crunches.

"True," I said. "Especially after the cops showed up."

"Oh, that's when it got good," she said.

"Good in what way?"

Skully dug around inside the Doritos bag. "I hate how they fill the bag with air, just to make you think you're getting more." She tilted it into her mouth. "Anyway. I was on the roof, okay? And these emo kids come running over, all drunk and shit. They start throwing bottles at people. They end up denting Brent's hood, just as he's driving off. It was freaking hilarious. We still don't know who did it."

"Check out my battle wounds." I showed her my arm.

Brent gave me a long stare. He was sitting on a skateboard so wide, it looked like he could surf waves with it.

"Nice kicks," he said in this whispery voice.

I stared down at my own double-knotted Converse high tops.

Skully smacked Brent. "Shut up. What's wrong with his shoes? You can't knock a classic."

"They're too clean. Looks like he bought them yesterday." The metal studs in his chin caught the light as he smirked.

Skully was on a roll. She said the cops shut down the

party, a total invasion of her rights. They set up a road-block at the end of her street. As the cars filed out, they checked IDs. A couple of people spent the night in jail.

"Listen," she said, squeezing my arm so tight, I lost circulation. "This girl took my dad's Hummer before the whole cop thing happened. She only has her learner's permit."

"You let her borrow it?"

"She said she'd be right back," said Skully. "Anyway. She takes off, doing like eighty on the expressway. The cops finally catch up and pull her over. My parents say she stole the car. I mean, she drove it without my dad's permission, but come on."

"What happened to the car?"

"A tow truck brought it back this morning."

"Yo," Brent said. "Is she still in the slammer?"

"God," said Skully, lighting a bidi.

"Isn't that dangerous? Smoking in a gas station?" I asked.

"I'm living on the edge," she said. "Just like Aerosmith."

"So when's the next party?" I asked. I needed to keep gathering info, try to get to the real criminal and bypass Morgan and Skully.

"Not at my place," said Skully, blowing a smoke ring. "Somebody scratched up the kitchen counter and the cleaning woman ratted on me."

"Are you going to that art show in Wynwood?" Brent asked her.

"You know I hate that kind of shit," she said. "All those

freaking pretentious art whores judging me with their hundred-dollar T-shirts from Tokyo."

This comment surprised me. Skully's family was loaded, but she dressed like a skate rat. Maybe it was part of her disguise.

"So what's up with you and Morgan?" Brent asked me.

"We're friends," I told him. "That's all."

"That's not what I heard."

"Well, you heard wrong," I said.

"Admit it. Her body is slamming. You totally want to hit that, right?"

What was the deal with this guy?

Skully made a face. "I really don't need to hear about your jerk-off fantasies right now."

He let out his jackhammer laugh. I felt like punching him.

I glanced across the station. An attendant was waddling toward us, belly straining against his polyester shirt.

"*No fumar*," he said, wagging his fat fingers.

"No problemo," Skully said, flicking the bidi into the street.

The attendant's face glistened with sweat. "Out," he bellowed.

We got up and moseyed across the intersection, taking our time. Brent skated ahead, propelling himself forward with deep, sweeping kicks. I turned around and the attendant was still there, making sure we didn't come back.

As we approached the school parking lot, the post-lunch herd had wandered back to campus.

"Only ninety minutes to go. That's, like, a whole mix tape, both sides," Skully said. "What class have you got now, Brent?"

"A.P. Biology," he said.

"That blows."

Brent stepped on the board and it bounced into his hand. Damn. I wished I still had my wheels and decks. I hadn't skated in years.

"Listen to Ms. Special Ed," said Brent. "For your information, it rocks. We're dissecting pig fetuses today."

Skully groaned. "You freak. Catch you later." She skipped off toward the classrooms.

Brent reached into his backpack and pulled out a heap of flyers. "Want to give me a hand?"

A hand. Yeah, right. I'd give him a fist. Straight into his metal-studded chin.

"Sure," I said.

"Thanks, bro," he said without looking up. Okay. So now we were buddies? He moved to a Jeep, slid a flyer under the windshield wiper.

"Is this for the thing in Wynwood?" I asked.

"Yeah. I promised Morgan that I'd pass these around. It's for her lameass art show," he said, shoving a handful at me. "Last time she gave me a shitload of flyers, I dumped the entire pile at Sweat Records. She didn't know the difference, bro."

We spent a few minutes tucking flyers into windshields. Brent had it down to a science: one in each corner of every window.

I slipped a flyer in my pocket, though I'd already memorized the gleaming, bold-faced font, the vector graphics rendered in Photoshop (an anime space girl with massive boobs).

"Stay away from Morgan," he said, all of a sudden.

"Look. Nothing happened. Besides, I'm not into her. I mean, she's hot or whatever, but I don't—"

I scanned the picnic benches and saw Morgan walking toward the trees near the tennis courts. This is where she usually hung out at lunch. She caught my stare and quickened her step.

Brent leaned closer. "She's bad news. Watch. She'll end up in jail, like that guy she's always with."

"What guy?" I asked.

"Finch and his boys. The e-tards were rolling, like, in front of everyone downstairs at Skully's, having a cuddle puddle on the floor."

He said this like it was no big deal.

"Where did they get the X?" I asked, trying to sound casual. "Can we get some?"

Brent raised an eyebrow. "I didn't know you liked to party like that."

"Forget it. I'll catch you later." I bumped past him.

Morgan saw me coming and kept up the fastwalk.

"Wait a sec," I called out, half-jogging across the grass.

"No running," said Mr. Pitstick. He slouched against the wall, a whistle dangling around his neck like he was some kind of food coach. When I ignored him, Mr. Pitstick blew the whistle. No doubt, he'd been waiting to do that all day.

Morgan didn't stop. I found a tennis ball on the ground and beamed it at her. It bounced near her feet and stuttered across the tennis court. She untangled herself from her iPod, still playing the depressing soundtrack of her life. "Aim a little higher next time."

"If you slowed down, my aim would improve," I said, catching up with her.

She stuck out her lower lip and puffed her bangs. God, she was hot. Her eyes were smudged so dark, it seemed like she was peering through a hole.

"I'm sorry. Do I know you? Oh, it's coming back to me now." She pushed me. Hard. "You really think you're special, don't you?"

"What?"

"When I first met you, I thought you were different. But I must've been on crack because you're just like all the other assholes in this school."

"Morgan, chill. What are you talking about?"

She shot me a look and all the molecules in my body vaporized. "Everybody knows."

"Knows what?"

"Do I have to spell it out?"

"Spell what out?" I asked.

"Would you please shut up?" Her eyelashes were wet.

"I can't stand the sound of your voice right now." Morgan wiped her face on her sleeve.

"Can we talk for a second?"

"I think you've done enough talking."

"What do you mean?"

"You told everyone."

"Told them what?" I shouted.

"That we slept together."

"I didn't say that. Who said that?"

"Maybe this will refresh your memory," she said, brandishing her cell phone.

I squinted at the picture on the screen: me and Morgan, locked in an embrace. From that angle, it looked like she wasn't wearing a top, but it was just her arm in the way. I racked my brain, trying to figure out when it was snapped. Probably at Skully's party. From the message details that appeared as she scrolled down, the picture was sent to a hundred different phone numbers.

"Who sent that picture?" I asked.

"Obviously, you did. It came from your cell."

"Look." I shoved the phone at her. "You can scroll through all my photos, if you want."

She waved my hand away. "Do you think I'm stupid? You deleted it, obviously."

"But I dropped my phone, right? Somebody must've taken that picture and sent it out. I'm sorry this happened. It sucks. But I swear, I had nothing to do with it."

I could feel the stares burning into my back.

Now I had what my little sister would call a rep-yoo-tay-shun.

"You know what? You're a terrible liar," Morgan said, walking away.

If only she knew.

PART TWO

11 Dirty Laundry

The rest of the day passed in a blur. At home, I logged onto Facebook and noticed that my friend count had gone down. I scanned through all the names and Morgan didn't show up. She must have deleted me. God, this hurt on so many levels. I glanced at the rubber band that she'd slipped on my wrist. I never took it off.

Out of desperation, I typed her name into the search box, but when I found her profile, it said something like, *Morgan only shares with friends...*

In other words, I'd been blocked.

I scrolled through her so-called online community and clicked on Brent's profile. Just looking at it made me sick. I kept going down the list, all those meaningless names and crappy photos, searching for the guy with the ecstasy connection.

On the next page, I saw my own face.

I stared at the picture. Judging from the washed-out pixilation, it looked snapped from someone's cell phone. I blinked at it for a few seconds, then clicked on the profile.

Whoever made the fake Aaron profile had cut and pasted all of my interests from the original page, down to my stupid misspelling of the band Evanesence. The only thing they got wrong was my age, which they listed as 100. My fingers shook as I clicked on PHOTOS and found a picture of my smiling parents, stolen from my cell phone.

The fake Aaron didn't have many friends, just a couple girls from English class. After gawking at all those animated graphics wishing me a happy hump day, Jewish new year, and Friday the 13th, I clicked back to my real page. This was so messed up. I mean, who would do something like this? And why?

There was a new message in my Facebook inbox. The subject line said, *What u looking 4*, sent by someone whose name was just a random series of letters: HIOFCR. Maybe it was spam, an automated message sent by a robot. I clicked on it anyway.

A new profile appeared, someone without a picture. Still, I noticed that the mystery profile was a male who lived in Miami. The message itself said, "October 31," which was just a few weeks away. "Tamiami Trail. (US HWY 41)."

On a hunch, I Googled the text. The first thing I

found was a Wikipedia entry. Turns out the Tamiami Trail crossed into Shark Valley, the northern edge of Everglades National Park. Beneath a bleary photo of an alligator, the caption said, *Wildlife sightings are common along the trail, which has no fences.*

I scribbled down the info. Then I changed my password.

Status: UNSENT
To: LadyM
From: Metroid
Subject: Give Me Novacaine

Dear Morgan,

Do you ever write letters in your notebook and retype them as e-mails? Would you believe I'm desperate enough to try it? I'd have to answer "yes." Plus my pen is bipolar or something.

I hope Pitstick doesn't make me read out loud. Today he's wearing one of those tent-sized "pleather" jackets, the kind that's always on sale at Burlington Coat Factory because nobody wants to wear a dead cow.

Pitstick: Blah blah blah.

Me: zzzzzzzzzzzzzzzzz

He always writes three rows of notes on the board.

Three. Separate. Rows.

When he runs out of room, he just squishes it together, writing more useless crap with that ugly green marker. It hurts, just staring at it.

We are reading about the Trojan Horse (1000x better than The Odyssey). This morning, he's making us watch a stupid DVD: "The Crucible of Civilization." It wouldn't suck so bad if he didn't keep stopping and starting it, just to "enlighten" us with his brilliant commentary. He won't even turn the lights off so I can sleep.

OMFG. A girl just asked Pitstick if he believes in the Lost City of Atlantis.

"That's a good question," he said.

When teachers say, "That's a good question," it means they don't know the answer.

I'm pressing the "save" button in my head. I need to remember this so we can talk about it later. You are, like, the smartest person I know. We'll probably have another one of our epic conversations... if you ever talk to me again.

You said that your family tree was rotten. I'm still trying to figure that out. I don't want to psychoanalyze you about it. But when you mentioned that your stepmom calls you fat, I couldn't believe it. Shit. I just think that's so wrong. And so untrue.

I want to know everything about you.

I want to kiss your branches and your leaves.

I am so sorry about what happened at Skully's party. Things got out of control. We were all pretty wasted, I guess. For the record, I didn't send that picture.

And you're not fat. Trust me. You're perfect. Well, nobody's perfect.

Especially not me.

—A.

———

After class the following Friday, I was hanging out at the Tombstone. As usual, Nolan Struth was there, taking up space. This time, he was by himself. When he saw me, he got this bugged-out look on his face, like he was scared.

"Did you find the plutonium? For your time machine or whatever," I said, lighting up a bidi.

Nolan leaned back in his wheelchair. He squeezed his eyes shut, like that could make me disappear. "I'm not supposed to talk to you."

"Why the hell not?" I was kind of surprised. And a little hurt. "You're talking to me now."

He didn't even crack a smile. Not that he smiled much, anyway. "They told me not to."

"Who's 'they'?"

"The whole school."

Okay. That narrowed it down.

"What exactly did the whole school tell you?" Sometimes it took a little sentence mapping to get through to Nolan.

"They said you're acting different, and it's really weird."

"Do you buy that?" I asked carefully.

Nolan looked down at the pavement, where the Spirit Club had left one of their support messages for the football team:

.50 WINS!!!

The chalk letters were smeared with sneakerprints.

Somebody had added a dot in front of the five, making it seem like half a win.

"I think you've changed," he said.

It was my senior year. Why couldn't I change? Or was everybody so caught up in the social chess game, we weren't allowed to rearrange the pieces? Sometimes I wanted to flip the board upside-down. Let gravity decide the rest.

"People have been saying stuff about you," Nolan said.

"What kind of stuff?"

He didn't answer. Instead, he said something totally bizarre, in true Nolan style:

"You can't just go hanging out with girls."

"Yeah?" I said.

The bidi had shriveled down to nothing. All I had left were used matches. Real used ones, not the magic-markered kind. I flicked the bidi on the concrete. It landed in the pile of cigarette butts—some half-smoked, some rimmed with lipstick.

"Maybe I like it," I told him. "Did you ever think of that? Besides. It's my personal right to hang with whoever I want."

"Not those girls," he said.

Out of everyone I'd met at Palm Hammock, Nolan Struth was the last guy I expected to go around judging people. God knows he put up with enough judgment on his own time.

"Well, good luck with the plutonium," I muttered, turning back toward the classrooms. I didn't mean to sound harsh, but that's the way it came out. Nolan cringed, as if I'd punched him in the stomach.

Maybe it was true, what he said.

I had changed.

———————

I called Morgan and apologized in a voicemail. For what, I wasn't really sure.

At first, she wouldn't pick up. I probably called, like, five times. It was sort of stalkerish, I admit. When she finally answered, I held the phone to my stereo. Played her a few tracks by her favorite bands. She listened to every song. Then she listened to me.

"That picture was on my phone, okay? That doesn't mean I sent it."

"I know," Morgan said quietly.

"When I find out who did it, trust me, I will destroy them in so many ways."

"My hero."

I imagined her rolling her eyes. Yeah, it was official. I wasn't anybody's hero. That's for damn sure.

"So ... we're friends, right?" she asked.

Friends.

I'd never hated a word so much in my life.

"Yeah," I said. "We're friends."

"Good. Because this enemy stuff is getting old."

It was kind of weird, talking like that again. Weird in a good way. No awkward silences, where you wonder if the other person put the phone down to take a leak. With Morgan, I could blab about anything from Bigfoot to weapons of mass destruction.

I still couldn't believe we'd made out. Blame it on the booze. Now I started to realize that all the guys at Palm Hammock ignored Morgan, who usually left the cafeteria at lunch to sit by herself, under a tree with a book. She was one of those weird popular girls, who everybody knows but nobody really is close to. Lots of "friends" but no *real* friends, it seemed. I secretly thought she was the hottest girl in school. They just didn't get it. For some strange reason, neither did she.

Morgan said she'd meet me later at the gallery in the Design District, which wasn't far from my apartment. I could ride my bike, which was probably a smart idea.

Outside, I heard Mama Pigeon fluttering around. Dad used to call pigeons "sky rats." I yanked back the curtain. The chicks had finally hatched. They sat there, alone. Their beaks opened wide, like singers in a silent choir.

"What's up?" I whispered, as if they could actually talk back.

In this building, people passed in the hall without talking. On the rare occasions I waved hello, they looked the other way. It totally creeped me out. We were living under one roof, yet I knew more about the pigeons than my next door neighbors.

To be totally honest, I was kind of lonely. My little sister had more of a social life than me. During the past few weeks, I'd seen less and less of Mom. She left Post-It notes all over the apartment in her jittery handwriting:

Toilet is on the fritz. Jiggle chain in tank. Make sure everything goes down.

Keep air conditioner on 75. Call me if it freezes up.

Her latest:

We need to talk about your grades.

I crumpled it up and threw it away.

Nothing left to do except practice my magic. I tried the levitation trick, but my feet wouldn't stay balanced. I ended up falling on my ass over and over again. After a while, I gave up. I really needed to get a life.

I jogged downstairs and threw my dirty laundry in the machine. Someone had already taken my jeans out of the dryer and tossed them in a wrinkled pile. Nice. I scooped up my faded Levis and smoothed them out, but they'd shrunk beyond recognition, the hole and worn part enlarged and clearly visible. This is what my world had become: shrunken laundry. How sad is that?

The machine thumped like a metronome, putting me into a trance. After a while, I couldn't listen to it anymore. I climbed the stairs and stumbled over the chewed-up carpet. I hadn't explored this part of the building yet.

At the top of the stairway, beside a fuse box with a mess of wires snaking out of it, a door dangled on its hinges. The other side was draped with Christmas lights. I stepped onto the roof. Airplanes roared overhead. Pigeons clustered against the railings, tucking themselves in for the night. I searched for my favorite pigeon, Wendy, in the flock, but I couldn't find her black-and-white cookie pattern.

This place was kind of chill. Somebody had even set up a little table and a deck chair. I sank into it. There was a six-pack of Presidente nearby. What the hell? Since I didn't see anybody around, I cracked open a can. Then I saw something that blew me away. Mom's earrings, the ones shaped like teddy bears to match her wacked-out scrubs. Had she been sneaking beers on the roof? The idea was so freaking weird, I couldn't wrap my head around it. Guess I wasn't the only one with a secret.

I closed my eyes and listened to the surf sounds of traffic. I hadn't been sleeping well, for obvious reasons. Now my internal clock was totally screwed up. Just as I started to drift off, my cell phone vibrated against my skin.

"It's starting. Where are you?" Morgan asked, her voice buried in a swirl of cackling laughter and car horns.

"On my way," I told her.

I glanced across the roof, which was littered with empty beer cans. The Christmas lights blinked on and off. As I headed toward the door, I spotted something crumpled in the corner. A rag. Peering closer, I realized it was a pigeon. The wings were splayed above its head, and the feathers, dappled with blood, were black and white.

12   The Ringmaster

Maybe gulping down a warm Dominican beer and hopping on a ten-speed wasn't a smart idea. As I squinted into the bleary distance, I tried to concentrate on the buildings ahead of me, the cartoony, hand-painted signs advertising everything from car parts to human hair.

I pedaled faster.

Morgan's directions made no sense. She said to meet at a place on northwest Twenty-third Street, but all I saw were junkyards. Something hard and sharp bounced off my shoulder. I winced. On the corner, a pack of kids on low-riding bikes took turns chucking rocks at me. None of them looked bigger than my little sister.

"Hey, man," said a boy with a Marlins cap. "You got a flat." He grinned, showing the spaces between his teeth.

"Thanks," I said as another rock sailed over.

I ducked and lost control of the bike. Then I tumbled onto the pavement, scraping my knees and elbows. The kids clapped and laughed. They were still laughing when I twisted my handlebars back in place, hopped on, and veered down a side street just to get away.

I had shredded a hole in my jeans, but for once I was in luck, because this looked like the spot. A crowd had gathered in front of a wall decorated with a mural: gigantic meat cleavers and steak knives. I chained my bike in front of a power station across the street, listened to the buzz of electricity, and started looking for Morgan.

She wasn't at the table near the gallery entrance, where hipster chicks in motorcycle boots and neon tights waited in line for booze. I asked if they'd seen Morgan. Nobody paid attention to me. Could I blame them?

"Who's asking?"

I recognized that twangy Southern accent. Finch, the guy from Skully's party. He never stopped smiling. His stupid mustache would put Dali to shame.

"A friend," I told him.

Finch's smile tightened.

We marched through the gallery's cavelike entrance, which was draped with strips of plastic. Inside, I found Morgan talking to her unstable ex-boyfriend, Brent.

"Do you think anyone would notice if I smoked a joint?" he asked.

Morgan giggled. "You crackhead."

"What if I smoked a cigarette at the same time?" he said. When he spotted me coming, he scowled. I kept looking at the studs in his chin. If only I had a crowbar.

"Aaron. You made it," Morgan said.

Normally, I'd be getting a little freaked out. I couldn't handle parties, and these people made me feel stupid, like I could never say the right thing. But as long as Morgan was around, I'd be okay.

"Yeah. Well, I almost got assaulted by a gang of ten-year-olds on bikes," I said.

Finch barged between us. He kissed Morgan on the cheek. "You know this guy?"

"Doesn't everybody?" she said. "He's my hero."

"Is that so?" Finch stared.

"She's kind of exaggerating," I said.

"Finch," the guy said, sticking out his hand. Was that his first name or his last?

"Yeah. I remember. You were at Skully's party."

Finch took off his hat and bowed. His hair was a tangle of reddish-brown snarls. He was older than us. Maybe in his midtwenties. He had a few crinkly wrinkles around the eyes, as well as freckles.

"Walk," he said, steering Morgan toward a metal staircase.

"I am walking," she said.

He pushed her forward. "I would say you're sort of shuffling."

"Don't touch me." Morgan jerked away.

They wandered down a hallway on the second floor, and Brent and I followed them. The air was sweltering. My T-shirt clung to my back. "Where the hell are we going?" I asked.

Finch jingled a set of keys and unlocked a door. Inside was another musty room with a cement floor. The walls swarmed with hundreds of postcard-sized doodles.

"Welcome, kids," he said, extending his arms.

I squinted at a drawing of a topless girl, splattered with something dark and gluey, like chocolate syrup. Her arms and legs were all twisted, her bazooka-sized boobs swelling out of the frame. It was scary as hell.

"Stop staring at my breasts," said Morgan, sneaking up behind me.

"That's you?" I blinked.

"Part of me," she said. "Wanna buy some art?"

"How much?"

She grinned. "Ten."

"Ten bucks?"

"No. Ten thousand. But for you, I'll take a rain check." She tore one of the drawings off the wall—a girl morphing into a tree—and stuffed it in a plastic baggie. "*Gracias*," she said, handing it to me.

I tucked it into my messenger bag. Did Morgan really see herself like that, with her body all out of proportion?

"Smells like dogs in here," said Brent. "Your place is in serious need of AC. It's hot as balls."

Finch led us toward the back. We snuck behind a curtain that separated the gallery space from the "sitting area," as Morgan called it. She collapsed onto a saggy couch and kicked her feet near an industrial-strength fan.

"This isn't helping. It's just throwing hot air around," she said.

"Quit your bitching," said Finch, pulling back another curtain. I got a glimpse of pizza boxes and sleeping bags and finally put two and two together. Not only did Finch own the gallery, he lived here.

Finch returned with a plate loaded with white powder. "You want K or coke?"

Brent clapped his hands. "Decisions, decisions."

Morgan didn't say anything. She just stared at the plate.

Brent was the first to take a hit. He leaned in and sniffed a line. Could be cocaine or ketamine, a pet tranquilizer used by vets. The cops had prepped me, but I couldn't tell the difference. I'd have to watch and see how he reacted. Either he'd space out or talk nonstop.

"What about you?" Finch jabbed a finger at me.

"Ladies first," said Morgan. "It's my opening night, remember?"

Was she joking?

"You don't have to," I said.

I didn't really expect her to do anything, but she pulled back her hair, bent forward and bumped a pile. Then she flopped against the couch and sighed. I watched her chest heave beneath her flimsy tank top.

"Next," said Finch, passing the plate.

"I'm good," I told him. This was so shady. I'd never even seen someone snort coke before. It kind of grossed me out.

"He's the guy you mentioned?" Finch asked Morgan. Something in his voice had shifted, all jokes and smiles gone.

Morgan said, "Let's have a race," and jogged around the room.

"Crazy girl," said Brent. He closed his eyes.

Finch glared at me. Shit. Things were getting out of control. I was in for it now.

"You interested in something else?" he asked.

I studied my fingernails. "Maybe."

"Who you buying for?" Finch asked. He fished out a pack of Camels and lit up.

"Just me."

Finch blew smoke at the ceiling. "This ain't how I do business."

There was no doubt in my mind. Finch was the supplier. The alpha dog. The shot caller. Whatever you wanted to call him. This was the guy. Now I had one plan: bring him down so Morgan and Skully didn't get dragged along with him.

"It's all good," Morgan said, skipping behind the couch. She slung her arms around my neck. "He's cool."

Finch didn't look convinced. He took a long drag, then flicked the cigarette across the floor, scattering a trail of sparks. "What's your name again?"

"Aaron."

He shook his head. "How about mollies? I got some real nice pills from Amsterdam. Not too speedy."

"Does a body good," said Brent, snickering. "Unless they're meth bombs."

Finch shot him a dirty look.

"Give me a jar." That's what the cop told me to say. He even gave me the cash, which they had photocopied.

"Why so much?" Finch narrowed his eyes.

"Some for now, some for later."

"Okay," he said. "I gotta take a drive first."

We exchanged phone numbers, then made a plan to meet in the parking lot at Pollo Tropical, a local fast food joint, in an hour. Just when everyone started to breathe easy, Finch took hold of my shoulder.

"You a cop?" he asked, keeping his gaze locked.

I faked a laugh. "Are you?"

Finch didn't look away.

"What time is it?" asked Morgan, breaking the silence.

"Time to jet," I said, stumbling away from the couch. I grabbed Morgan's hand to help her up and she beamed at me.

"You can let go now," she said.

But I didn't ever want to let go.

13 Pit Stop

Finch yanked back the curtain. On the other side, a crowd of bored-looking girls had gathered. He switched gears again, turning on his megawatt smile. This seemed odd. Was he the alpha dog or just a foot soldier? It could go either way.

My beer buzz had worn off. At that point, I could've used another. Not that I was supposed to be drinking in the first place. I felt like the living dead.

I noticed Skully in her heart-shaped glasses, standing in the corner, smoking her cloves. She smiled and did this weird little curtsey, like a queen in an old movie.

"Hey, Double A." She pulled me into a hug. "Let's dance," she said, twirling around. Her skirt puffed up, giving everyone a glimpse of her polka-dotted panties.

"I don't dance."

"Sure, you do," Skully said. "Just go like this. Feel the beat." She swung her shoulders back and forth.

I tried to mimic her movements, but I stumbled all over the place. Skully laughed. "Loosen up, Double A," she said. "God, you should take yoga or something."

Morgan came out and sort of sleepwalked over to us. She pulled me away, and then we were swaying together. We held each other like that for a while, our feet perfectly still.

The warehouse could've burned down in flames. I wouldn't have noticed.

Then, for no reason, she pushed me away, and I was standing there alone again, looking foolish.

The girls, Brent, and I ran down the metal stairs, back into the cavernous room where the lights had dimmed. Video games flickered on the wall. People spread out on the floor, playing vintage Metroid, the final battle, where the player's helmet comes off and you realize that inside the metal suit, the hero, Samus, is a girl.

"The sickest 2-D platform game of all time," said Brent. "I'll take the old-school NES over the Xbox. Those 360 games give me a freaking headache."

As he blabbed on about alien life forms, my mind shifted back to Finch and the deal. How long would it take? I didn't know how this stuff worked. The most hard-core thing I'd done was buy weed off Collin's brother.

"Shall we battle?" Brent asked.

"I'm kinda out of practice."

He grabbed a joystick. "I'll be gentle."

I hadn't played the game since junior high, but I remembered all the cheat codes and tricks, like how to jump through walls. Brent was impressed. "You've got to teach me some tricks, man. You're, like, the old-school master."

I shrugged. "It's all good."

"You've got a lot of rage inside you."

This took me by surprise. "You think?"

"It's cool, man. My dad used to beat the shit out of me and I'd hide in my room all day, playing Quake with my friends online. Just pretending I was fragging him."

When Brent told me this, I couldn't help feeling sorry for him. I mean, I still hated the kid. But it was pretty obvious he had problems of his own.

Didn't everybody?

When we stepped outside, Finch had already disappeared. The girls were getting restless. Morgan wanted to walk to a gas station for a Red Bull. Skully kept dancing around, pretending to karate-chop me in the face. We squeezed into Brent's car, a black-and-white Mini Cooper that he called Nigel because it's "the most British-sounding name" he could think of.

He sped down Biscayne Boulevard, swerving between lanes. I looked at him and wondered if he was really okay to be driving. I still wasn't sure what he had in his system. Skully stared dreamily out the passenger window. Morgan bounced in the back seat, her long legs sprawled across my lap. Not that I was complaining.

We pulled into the Shell station near my place. It felt strange coming here with the group of them.

Brent jumped out. "Want anything?"

"I'm good," I told him.

As soon as he took off, a truck pulled up, blasting rap anthems.

"Check out the yo-bros," said Skully.

The guys in the truck were checking us out, too. One of them leaned out the backseat, a musclehead in a Miami Hurricanes jacket. He tossed a Fanta bottle, which bounced against the driver's side door, spewing an orange geyser. Talk about gross.

"Ugh. That is so wrong," Morgan said.

The guy who tossed the bottle was hooting with his buddies. I could tell they were wasted and looking for a fight.

"Just ignore those assholes," I said. "It's not even worth it."

Skully popped up through the sunroof. "You homeboys want to mess with me?" she shouted. "Nice rims. What is that? Compensation? You got short man syndrome?"

The girls cackled over Skully's joke. I'd heard that one before. In junior high, people never ran out of one-liners: "Hey Aaron. You need cash? Or are you a little short? Hey Aaron. Do you smoke weed because it makes you high?" I used to drink these chalky protein shakes, hoping it would kick start my growth hormones. Maybe it did. Or maybe Morgan was different. For the first time in my life, I didn't feel small.

"I would define it as vertically challenged," Skully added in the voice of a documentary narrator.

The yo-bros stared. One of them yelled, "Hey. Are you a dude or a chick?"

I caught a glimpse of Skully's face, the hurt registering, and I wanted to pound the guy into the concrete. Sure, her hair was kind of butchy, but I would never mistake Skully for a dude.

"Fuck you," Skully yelled.

"Thanks, but I'll pass," he said, igniting more guffaws from his crew. He got out and strutted toward us.

"Enough," I said, climbing out. "You guys need to step away from the car and take it easy."

"'Step away from the car'?" he said. "What are you? Highway Patrol?"

That's when I slammed my fist into his jaw. Clocked him so hard, my knuckles popped. Almost instantly, he managed to scramble back on his feet. That's the thing about drunks. They were always the ones to shake off a fight or a car crash.

"Oh shit," said Brent, racing toward the car. "Get in, will you?"

I glanced back at the convenience store and saw the cashier, a straggly blond in a Playboy cap, punching buttons on a phone. Time to leave.

When I hopped in the backseat, the girls were freaking out. Morgan started to sob, and Skully stroked her hair.

Brent hit the gas. We peeled down a side street, past a block of construction sites, the cranes stabbing the horizon.

Brent pulled into a twenty-four-hour bank and spun out. When I reminded him about the deal with Finch, he laughed.

"He runs on Cuban time," said Brent.

"He's Cuban?" I asked.

"No. I mean the guy's always late. Don't sweat it."

Morgan groaned. She slumped forward, dropping her head between her knees. I was starting to get worried about her.

"Hey, sleepy. Wake up," I said, ruffling her hair.

She didn't budge.

"Didn't she just knock back an energy drink?" Skully asked.

"Yeah," I said. "Among other things."

"What's that supposed to mean?"

"We were with Finch earlier—"

"Aaron, what did she take?"

"I don't know."

"How come you don't know?" Skully said, her voice rising.

"Because I don't, okay? Ask Brent. I saw him snort a line."

"Only a hit," he said. "Not enough to put her in a K-hole."

"Maybe she did another line or something else when we weren't looking?"

I unsnapped Morgan's army knapsack and rummaged

through it. I pulled out two Band Aids, a pair of nylon footies, lip gloss in Matador Red, rolling papers, a Lifestyles Tuxedo condom, a Hello Kitty pen with the cap chewed off, a digital camera, a South Dade Library card, and a half-melted Jolly Rancher lollipop with gobs of hair sprouting from it.

"Here we go." I found a jar, about an inch long and the same murky orange as a medicine bottle. There was still a smidge of powder left in it. That must have been it.

I tugged Morgan out of the car in the bank parking lot. She teetered backward, like she was going to fall, then collapsed against me. I dragged her along, as if she'd morphed into a zombie, her wide eyes fixed in some other time zone. Then she threw up on the sidewalk. Even the noise was enough to make the back of my throat tickle. When she finished, she just wiped her mouth. No big deal.

As we staggered towards the alley, a security guard hustled over. He didn't look happy.

"Is there a problem?" he asked.

"No, sir," I said.

The guard scowled at Morgan. "Has your friend been drinking?"

Skully slid between us. "Too much caffeine."

"You guys have some identification?" the guard asked.

Skully fumbled around in her tote bag. I pulled out my wallet. Morgan wasn't exactly helping. In fact, she was sliding around on the sidewalk without lifting her feet.

"Can I talk with you alone for a second?" I asked him.

"We can discuss it right here. Your girlfriend," he said, gesturing to Morgan, "is going straight to the drunk tank. She'll spend the night there. Sleep it off, you know? Sober up."

"Her parents are going to kill me. Please. Just let me talk to someone," I said.

The guard stepped closer. No doubt hoping to get a whiff of booze on my breath. "Who do you want to talk to?"

I could've called the lead officer, but what the hell would I say? I glanced back at Skully, who had taken this opportunity to jump in the car.

"Get in, man!" Brent hollered.

Like an idiot, I grabbed Morgan's hand and started running.

The security guard was swearing, then I couldn't hear him anymore. They guy hadn't gotten a good look at our IDs; we might be okay. I shoveled Morgan in the rear door. Before I even slammed the door, Brent peeled out. The brakes squealed as we lurched onto the highway.

Skully smacked him. "This is so messed up. The last time I went to jail was never. And just so you know … there's no frigging way I'm doing this again. Everything else was rad, though."

Morgan slumped against me. "Think I'm going to puke," she mumbled.

"You already did that," I told her. "We've got to take you somewhere."

"Any ideas?" Brent asked.

"We could drive back to my place," said Skully.

"Forget it," he said. "That's too far away."

"Don't you live around here?" Morgan slurred.

"Yeah, but..." I mumbled.

My mom was a nurse. She would take one look at Morgan and know what's up. I checked the time on my cell. Maybe Mom was at work? I couldn't keep up with her crazy schedule. I wasn't even sure if she was home or not.

"Well?" Brent asked.

"Turn left at the light," I told him.

14 Crazy Good

We drove back to the apartment. I stretched the rubber band around my wrist and stared out the window, watching the headlights gobble up the dark. The girls were going to see my place, the dirty laundry, the mess, and wonder why I was camping in the living room.

I twisted the rubber band so tight, I lost circulation. By the time we pulled up to the apartment, I wondered if it was over. Finch had probably shown and left. I seriously doubted that he would wait.

"This is your place?" Skully asked. "I mean, you actually live here?"

I nodded.

"Sweet," she said.

Mom saw us as soon as we pulled up. It looked like

she'd just gotten back from the store or something. Now she stood there by the front door, hands on her hips, plastic bag hanging from one wrist. I was pretty sure she'd been drinking.

"What's the deal, mister?" she asked.

"Everything's cool, Mom," I told her. Another lie.

My oh-so-exciting Saturday nights were usually spent in front of the computer playing Call of Duty. No doubt Mom was curious about my new friends.

Morgan got out and wobbled next to me on the sidewalk. "This was definitely a journey," she said, slow and thick. She had started to come around again, shaking her head and saying things like, "I'm flailing hardcore."

"As mellow as you are," I said, "you can be a total psycho."

"I know," she whispered. "You better bust out some crazy good weed later."

Hopefully, Mom didn't hear that part.

"Wait," Morgan said. "This isn't your house, is it?"

Before I could make up an excuse, Mom beckoned us inside. "Well don't just stand there in the street like a bunch of damn criminals."

This was already getting embarrassing. I flinched. "Give us a second, okay?"

Mom looked at her watch. "Okay. Time's up."

"Oh, my god." Skully laughed like this was the funniest thing ever. "Your mom's hilarious, Double A."

"Now there's a lady with a sense of humor," Mom said.

"Damn straight."

"Can't pull the wool over your ice. That's what the Marx brothers used to say. You wouldn't know them. They were before your time."

"Are you kidding?" Skully said. "I freaking love the one where Harpo pretends to be Groucho in a mirror."

Mom grinned. "We're going to be good friends."

———————

The girls' heels clattered across the lobby's hardwood floors. Except it wasn't really hardwood. More like particle-board. This was majorly awkward.

"Watch for nails," said Mom. "They tore out the carpets last week."

"Smells rank," said Brent.

Upstairs, the stink was even worse: moldy wallpaper and leftover chicken chow mein. Mom unlocked the door. Everybody ran around, checking out the digs. Mom headed straight for the kitchen.

"Nice space. It needs more fabric elements, though. Where do you sleep?" Skully asked.

"Here." I unfolded my bed from the wall.

"Yo. That's old school," said Brent, flopping into it. "Did it come with the original stains?"

"Um. No. That's actually an old futon mattress. This place is just temporary … until my mom gets her nursing degree." I was rambling now. Beyond embarrassed.

Morgan looked more alive now. She was taking pictures

with her cell phone, documenting my laundry piles. Was there any chance that Finch would show up late? After what I'd seen tonight, I hated him more than ever. He had taken advantage of people at school and put Morgan in danger. She had called him "the only real" guy she knew, yet he was the biggest fake of all.

Well, maybe not the biggest.

Haylie came out of the bedroom, wearing my faded Andre the Giant T-shirt with the stretched-out collar. "Whoa," she said. "How come I wasn't invited?"

The girls oohed and aahed over my little sister. She kind of had that effect on people.

Haylie squeezed between them and started talking nonsense, as usual. "Your hair is so amazing," she said, petting Skully's spikes. "I've always wanted to shave the back of my head."

"Since when?" I asked.

Haylie kept going. "And the color is totally badass. Did you do it yourself?"

"Yes ma'am," said Skully. "The magic of Kool-Aid."

Great. Now my sister was getting styling tips from Skully.

"What's up, rocker? Look at you, dressing all scene," Morgan said, slipping her thumb inside the waistband of my too-tight and crumpled jeans.

"They shrank in the wash," I mumbled.

"Didn't your mom teach you how to do laundry?" She leaned forward, giving me a peek of her sunburned shoulders, among other things.

"We should style him," Skully announced, as if I wasn't even in the room.

Morgan grabbed a comb and had a field day with my hair. Not that I minded.

"All the better to hide your crying emo eyes," she said, raking my bangs.

Haylie laughed. "Your guys are way cool. Next time you have a makeover party, let me know."

Mom had broken out the skillet and started sizzling hotdogs. We ate off paper plates, camped around the TV. Skully sang along to the commercials on Telemundo, where everything was in Spanish except for words like *Whopper*.

Haylie kept playing with her cell phone the whole time. "My friend's picking me up," she said, dropping her plate next to the sink.

"Isn't it kind of late to go out?" I asked, but she ignored me.

Lately my sister was never around. Yeah, it was Saturday night. Haylie always had more of a social life than me. At the same time, I couldn't help wondering where she had disappeared to. And with who.

"Want to go outside for a puff?" Brent asked me.

Mom twitched an eyebrow. She'd never seen me smoke.

"Be back in a sec," I told her.

Brent pounded down the stairs. "Damn. How long you been living in this shithole?"

"Not long," I said. This was worse than I'd expected. Epic humiliation.

We slipped out the back door, into the sandy lot where the tenants parked their cars. A stray tabby was perched on top of Dad's pickup. When we stepped closer, the cat hurtled into the bushes.

"It must suck, not having your own room," Brent said.

"Thanks for reminding me." What the hell? This was all my mom could afford.

I checked my phone. Somebody had called without leaving a message.

"Recognize this number?" I asked him.

He gawked at it. "Nope. Doesn't look familiar."

"They called like, four times in a row," I said. "Probably when Morgan was having her moment or whatever. Are you sure it's not Finch?"

"Call them back. That's the only way to find out."

I hit redial. The phone rang and nobody answered, not even a machine.

When we got back inside, I found Morgan hunched in front of my laptop, pecking away. Shit. The lead officer never contacted me through e-mail, but there was plenty of other stuff I didn't want Morgan to find. I'd been Googling everybody's names from the whole damn school.

"Just checking my e-mail. Your mom said it was all good," she told me.

I bit my lip. The last time I logged online, I didn't clear

my history. Hopefully, Morgan wasn't the snooping type, but somehow I doubted it.

"Let's go to the roof," I said. A lame attempt at changing the subject. This entire evening had been an epic fail.

The girls squealed.

Mom clapped her hands and said, "I'm going to hit the sack. Just don't wake the neighbors, okay, mister?" She seemed weirdly okay with me having people over with no notice, especially given Morgan's loopiness when we arrived. Maybe she just felt better knowing where I was.

I lead the way, up into the stairwell. The steps creaked as we climbed past the busted fuse box. I kicked open the door and everybody checked out the glittering skyline.

"There's Wendy's. I heart their chili," said Morgan, snapping a picture.

Brent tried to light a cigarette, but the breeze snuffed it. "Looks like somebody got the party started," he said, kicking an empty beer can. "Let's do something."

"Aaron can do magic," said Morgan.

"Magicians are hot," Skully added.

Brent glared at me. "Aren't you a little old for card tricks?"

"I'm not big into cards," I told him.

"So what do you do?"

Okay. This was it.

I stepped a few feet away from them. Tilting my body at an angle, I balanced on tiptoe. Then I lifted up, raising my feet off the ground. The girls screamed. Brent hopped backward, stumbling over himself, and tried to act all cool, as if he wasn't scared shitless.

I couldn't believe it. Damn. I'd actually pulled off the levitation trick that I'd been practicing for months.

"Okay, okay," Brent said. "That was freaky. Now tell us how you did it."

Morgan clutched her chest. "I thought I was going to pass out. That was, like, real magic."

"'Real magic'? What the hell is that?" Brent was losing his cool now.

I thrust my arm in front of him. "Lay off, okay?"

"Oh, you're her boyfriend now?"

Morgan was looking at me, her lips slightly parted, inviting. And then I leaned in, slow, and covered her mouth with my own. We kissed and it wasn't like before. It was more like she was pulling something out of me, reaching down inside, and taking hold, tight. Her lip ring bumped against my teeth. When she finally slipped away, I heard brakes squealing on the boulevard, pigeons rustling all around, and my own quick gasps. Now there was a sliver of gum sliding across my tongue, a little secret between us.

Brent flicked his cigarette on the ground and stomped it. Then he picked up one of the deck chairs and clattered it across the roof, knocking over empty beer bottles. A spray of broken glass flew in all directions. I looked at my ankle, at the tiny beads of blood dotting my skin. When I wiped them away, they popped up again.

"I'm getting the fuck out of here," Brent said.

He stormed back down the stairs. I was officially stuck. Mom was taking the truck later to work her shift. I had no form of transportation, no deal to report to the cops, and no time left. In other words, I had failed again. What a surprise.

I couldn't look at Morgan, although I felt her walking behind me, the warmth of her there, as if she knew too much. Skully cracked a joke about the "fragile male ego," but nobody laughed.

We made it back to the apartment. I went to the closet, grabbed a heap of blankets, and spread them on the floor. The girls stretched out like we were throwing a slumber party. Skully had already taken the bed, so I settled on the floor.

Morgan snuggled next to me. "Mr. Mystery," she whispered.

"You really scared me tonight," I whispered back. "Do you use that stuff a lot? I mean, the ketamine or whatever."

"It's a lot safer than the weight-loss pills my stepmom gave me."

"Pills? When was this?"

"Junior high."

"Shit. Are you still taking them?"

"Obviously not. Then my fat ass would still fit, you know... the size zero jeans I used to wear."

"For the record, you're not fat. How many times do I have to tell you? And who wears a size zero anyway? It's not even a number."

She traced the stubble along my jaw. "You're funny."

I waited to see what she'd do next. Soon she was snoring faintly, her chilly toes tucked against my own. I stayed awake, chewing the flavorless gum because my mouth felt too full. When I finally swallowed it, a trickle of sunlight had cut the room in half, the other side still bathed in shadow. And as I faded into sleep, I heard a familiar rustling: Wendy's orphaned chicks at the window, cooing in minor keys.

For some reason, I felt like I was the one who let them down.

15 Carnations

The bus was late, as usual. Morgan slumped on the bench, doodling in her sketchbook. I glanced down at her ballpoint cartoon: a raggedy dude with bugged-out eyeballs. I'd seen this guy at the coffeehouse formerly known as Joffrey's (hence vanquished by Starbucks). He always wore headphones and a rope-belted housecoat.

"That's the Cleric," I said, startling her.

"What? He's just this homeless freak I've been following on the beach," she said. "I might do a photo collage about him."

"I know that guy. Not personally. But I see the Cleric all the time. He always gets free coffee."

"Yeah," she said. "I've never seen him pay."

"I have this theory about him. He's actually a multibillionaire genius. He's, like, this computer-whiz inventor who struck it rich. He's only pretending to be crazy."

"And he's getting more perverted each day," she said, adding a garden hose (at least, I hope it was a garden hose), through which his lower body dribbled onto a patch of grass.

"You know, you're a really amazing artist," I told her.

"My drawings are crappy. And my parents aren't exactly thrilled with the idea of me studying art."

"I hear you," I said, nodding.

She returned to doodling in her sketchbook, as if the pen were surgically connected to her fingers. "They think I'm going to end up in a cardboard box by the MacArthur Causeway or something. They're totally in favor of me selling out." She kept looking at the drawing the whole time, talking to the Cleric instead of me.

"That sucks," I said.

"I was supposed to get this internship with that guy ... you know the one on Lincoln Road who makes Pop Art flamingoes?"

"Yeah?" I said, although I wasn't sure.

"Basically, I would be painting the flamingoes for him. You know, coloring inside the lines. But since I'd be working for free, my parents thought it was a waste of time. Then the weirdest thing happens. Right before I got fired, the bookstore asked me to do some lame-ass mural for them. I would've gotten paid and everything. They still want me to do it."

"See? You're official now."

"Not really. I'll probably blow it off."

"Are you crazy? This is, like, your big break. What's the problem?"

"I mean, it's a lot of work and I really don't feel like it," she said, scribbling out the Cleric's face. "Let's not talk about it anymore, okay?"

"Excuse me for believing in you."

"Sorry." Morgan capped her pen. "I didn't mean to come off like a bitch."

"That's all right. I didn't think you were. A bitch, I mean."

She leaned against me, and I forgot how to breathe.

"Makes some room, homies," said Skully, plopping down between us. She put on her heart-shaped glasses.

When the bus finally rumbled to the curb, a tide of people poured out, mostly old ladies with saggy, flesh-tinted stockings. As soon as they hit the sidewalk, they snapped open umbrellas, although the sky was smeared with just a few faint clouds, like chalk scribble.

"Guess they're allergic to sunlight," Morgan said, slamming her sketchbook shut.

We got on and found seats in the back.

"Man, I can't wait to be old," Skully said. "Then you can really hit the bitch-switch. Like, you'll go out to eat at four o' clock on Sunday, order the early bird special. And when your meatloaf comes out cold, you can yell at the waiter. Say things like, 'Make it snappy!'"

Morgan tore a page from her sketchbook and crumpled it into a ball. "Do you ever stop talking?"

"Geez, Louise. You've been bitchy all morning. Or should I say, 'witchy'?"

"Too bad I can't cast a spell on you. Then you'd finally shut up. And maybe," she said, turning to me, "I would know why you deleted me from your friends list."

I blinked. "What do you mean?"

"When I got online this morning, I noticed my friend count had changed. So I did a search for your name. Sorry if I sound like a cyber-stalker."

"I had a cyber-stalker last year. It was this kid I knew from grade school," Skully said.

Morgan scowled at her. "Anyway," she said, talking to the floor. "I noticed you changed your profile and I was like, What's up with that?"

I swallowed the knob in my throat. Nothing else to do but confess. "It's not me."

Morgan looked confused. "What do you mean?"

"Somebody made a fake profile," I explained.

"You're lying."

"No, I swear."

Morgan scrunched her eyebrows. I couldn't blame her for not believing. Whenever someone ends a sentence with, "I swear," you can bet they're lying.

"Check on Aaron's cell. It has Wi-Fi," Skully said.

"It does?" I flipped it open. The screen flickered to life. "You didn't know? What's the point of having a pimped-out phone if you can't surf the net?" Skully pushed buttons until a miniature version of Facebook popped up. "Fire away," she said, handing it back to me.

I typed my name, then a series of numbers and letters. It returned to the sign-on screen. I'd forgotten that I'd changed my password on the real page a few days ago. I tried again. When I finally reached the page, it looked different. Under Interests, it said, *Stealing your girl*. In the About You section, it said, *Fake ass poser*. I clicked on my picture.

NARC, it read in all caps.

I dropped the phone, which clattered on the floor and slid like a missile toward the back of the bus. I scrambled out of my seat. Skully beat me to it.

"Maybe they phished your password," she said, handing it back.

"What do you mean?" I asked.

"You click on a link and they hijack your profile. Are you getting a lot of spammy bulletins?"

"No. I didn't click on anything. I don't know how it got messed up."

"Oh, well. Just change your password."

"I did."

"Change it again." She laughed. "Don't freak out. It's no big deal."

Morgan touched my knee. "Any clue who did it?"

"Nada," I said. Another lie. Maybe it was her psycho ex-boyfriend sending those messages. Or some random person at school. Hell, it could've been Nolan Struth, traveling in his time machine.

"I don't think that's the profile I saw this morning. So which one is the real you?" she asked.

I got the same kind of feeling you get when you're crossing the street and a truck almost hits you.

"Neither of them," I said.

She pursed her mouth. For a minute, I zoned out, watching her lips close and open over that crooked smile. When I drifted back to earth, Skully was saying something about tech support.

"Send them a message. They'll kick off the imposter."

"Okay. Cool," I told her.

She waited. "Why don't you do it now?"

"Later," I said. "It's a pain in the ass."

"It's easy. Go to Inbox," she said, hovering over my shoulder.

"God, Skully. Give him some space," Morgan said.

"Listen," I said. "Check this out." I showed them the message, the one with the date and address. "Do you know who could've sent this to me?"

Skully squealed. "Oh, my god, Double A. You got an e-vite to a Halloween blowout in the Everglades? That's sick. Why didn't I hear about it?"

"Do you recognize this username?"

Skully shook her head. "Nope. But I am so there."

"Wait," I said. "There's nothing in the e-mail that mentions a party. It just says Tamiami Trail."

"It's on All Hallows Eve. What else would it be? Anyway, Morgan should know. She's the witch," Skully said.

Morgan turned to me. "Could be mildly amusing. You plan on going?"

"Hell no," I said.

"Well, now you have no choice," she said, smiling. "Because we're not having fun without you."

I sank down in my seat.

For the rest of the bus ride, the girls wouldn't stop talking about the "Glades party." If Skully posted a bulletin to all ten thousand of her closest "friends" in cyberspace, the entire school would show up.

The cops were planning a big bust. This meant an arrest of epic proportions—not just the dealer, but any kid from Palm Hammock who was caught smoking chronic or knocking back a few beers.

I was in this weird position, like I was Mr. Innocent, like I'd never touched weed or got wasted. The truth is ... I made lots of mistakes. Not because I was a bad person. There's all kinds of reasons why someone does a bad thing. Most of the time, we only see the surface of people—the face they put on at school, the shield, the battle armor.

Before I got to know the girls, I'd already made up my mind about them. At first, I thought they were just scene queens. I guess you could say I was judging, the way people had judged me. Now I was drifting on the other side, past the gates of social limbo. Except it felt more like Hades, the land of the dead.

16 Do Unto Others

When I ditched the girls, they gave me the third degree. I used the babysitting excuse, saying my little sister needed me. In a way, this was actually true. I stepped into the parking lot at the bookstore, took out my cell, and dialed the magic number. No dice. It didn't even ring once. I tried again. Same thing. I looked at the screen.

Searching for service.

I headed back inside and glanced around the store, at the bald dudes thumbing through sports magazines. I asked if I could use the phone behind the counter to make a local call.

"There's a pay phone at the Metro station. Go across the street," said the cashier.

I called the lead officer, then a Sunshine cab, and booked it out to Key Biscayne.

We weren't supposed to meet so soon (the less time I spend around cops, the easier it should be, staying undercover). He didn't ask why I called. Just materialized in the front row of the marine stadium, wearing his pleated khakis and aviator sunglasses.

The seats faced the bay, where bands used to perform on a floating stage. Graffiti was splashed across every part of it, from the crumbling skybox to the weed-infested orchestra pit.

I got there first and killed time, inspecting the aisles. On one of the seats, a tagger had sketched (with colored Sharpies, no less) a mural of Tom, the cartoon cat, hightailing it after Jerry the mouse. I never understood why people thought that shit was funny. Once in kindergarten, I raised my hand and told the teacher that I didn't get why ninety percent of kids' shows violated the Golden Rule, which she made us memorize and recite like robots. Ms. Kemp frowned. She asked if I knew the difference between the real world and make believe.

The cop was sweating. I wanted to jump in the waves and backstroke away from the questions I knew he'd ask.

"What have you found?" he asked, taking out a memo pad.

I told him about the date with Finch.

"So you bought a jar of X from this guy?" he asked, trying to be cool, speaking the lingo.

"Not exactly," I said.

"What happened?"

I could've lied. Or wiggle out by saying, "He flaked on me," which was exactly what I did.

"This is a real disappointment," he said.

I hung my head. God. Just rub it in.

"Did you get his number, at least?"

"Yeah." I took out my cell and searched the contact list. "Shit," I muttered. "Shit, shit, shit."

"What's the problem?"

"My phone died."

The cop sat there, saying nothing. "Died in what way?" he finally asked.

"It's not working."

He sighed. "Did you drop it somewheres?"

This was the only man I'd ever met who said *somewheres,* as if it were plural. As if there was more than one somewhere. I shrugged and told the truth for a change.

"Sorry. I kind of broke it."

He took the phone and slipped it into his shirt pocket. "I'll see if we can get it repaired. You can bet he's going to call again. Until then, we can get the paperwork started on a search warrant."

"Wait a minute. Whose house are you searching?" I asked.

"You already told me that this girl, Jessica Torres, has an operation going out of her parents' place."

"No. I mean, it's a party house. People hang out there.

I saw some things that night. But Skully is clean. In fact, she's almost straight-edge."

The cop put a hand on my shoulder. "Aaron. You're not protecting these kids, are you? No, you wouldn't do that. Because if you did, you'd be going to jail. I'd make sure of it. Do you understand?"

I nodded. An all-too-familiar sickness burned in my stomach. If I went to jail, who would watch out for Haylie? Not that was doing a real good job of it lately. Shit.

"Is that clear?" he repeated.

"Yes, sir."

"Good." He let go, but I could still feel his grip. "Now what about Morgan Bask—"

He couldn't even pronounce her name.

"Baskin," I said nice and slow for him.

"Right. She's the ex-ballerina. Floats between cliques. Easy on the eyes."

"What about her?"

"You told me that she's been dealing pot to her buddies. Because of her social standing, she might even be our alpha dog."

"Morgan isn't much of dealer. She just ends up giving it away to her friends."

"How do you know for sure? I mean, these popular kids ... you're not really part of their clique, are you?"

He goes right for it. My fatal weakness. My soft spot. My kryptonite.

"I'm not stupid," I tell him. "This is my school, okay? I see what's going on."

"So you witnessed a transaction," the cop said. He wanted to know: How much product? Where is it collected? Who handles the money?

I closed my eyes. When I opened them, the cop was still there, watching.

He jotted something down on a memo pad. "I'm going to look into those locations. Send a car out there."

"She's got a little brother," I said.

"What did you say?"

"Skully. I mean, Jessica. She's got a little brother. He's a diabetic."

"What age?"

"Midde school, I guess."

The cop put down his pen. "This complicates things." He stared at me. "You've got a younger sibling, too."

It took me by surprise. "What does my sister have to do with this?"

He kept his gaze pinned on mine. "You're not thinking of backing out, are you, friend?"

I swallowed hard.

"Because if you back out," he said, "we won't be there to protect you."

"Protect me? From what?" I stammered.

"Oh, let's see. You've already botched a deal with this guy, Finch. If he finds out that you're a snitch—and believe me, he will, if we don't take care of business soon—you're not the only one he'll be coming for."

No way could I let Haylie get dragged into this mess. So I lowered my head and said, "I'm not backing out."

"Whatever the case, I'm still going to keep watch on the addresses you mentioned. Maybe we'll hold off on the search until you can actually buy—"

"Finch is their supplier. Why don't you just search his place? I lost his number, but I think I can remember where we went to see him."

The cop stood. He smoothed the pleats in his pants.

"Take me there."

———————

"It's near a power station," I said.

We'd been driving around Wynwood in an unmarked car, a silver Corolla, for twenty minutes. As we passed the electric plant for the third time, I started to panic.

"Sure you know where it is?" he asked.

"Yeah. I chained my bike to the fence."

The cop smirked. "Well, it's not there anymore."

I stopped scanning the streets for my bike, which, no doubt, I'd never see again. The address was a blur. I couldn't get a sense of direction. It was starting to rain—slow, fat drops that Dad would have called "spitting."

"Okay. I'm going back now," he said. I could tell he was pissed.

He jerked the steering wheel and we turned back onto the street. We cruised around the hand-painted signs that reminded me of hieroglyphics—a high-heeled shoe, a pack of cigarettes, a floating soda can, a giant set of steak knives.

"There," I said.

The lead officer hit the brakes. He parked on the curb. Then we waited.

I stared at a burnt-out car in the adjacent lot. The driver's side window was shielded with tinfoil. Somebody was curled up in the back seat, a man resting on a blanket. I wondered if he was dead.

"Is that your guy?" the cop asked.

At first, I thought he meant the man in the car. Then I saw Finch in his stupid hat, creeping around the garbage cans wearing a wifebeater and boxer shorts. For some reason, he turned and looked at us. Maybe he was curious about the car. Or maybe it was an instinct left from prehistoric times.

"He sees me," I told the cop.

"Nah. We've got tints."

Finch started walking toward us.

"I'm going," I said.

The cop took off his sunglasses. "Where?"

"To do a little business."

"Not a smart idea," he said, but I was already messing with the door.

"It's cool." Actually, it wasn't.

"Okay. I'm going to take a drive and come back," he said.

"But my cell is busted. What if I need to call you?"

"Go," he said.

My fingers slipped on the handle, but somehow I managed to push it open. I got out and Finch came over.

"You disappeared the other night. I went out of my way and you didn't show," Finch said, like he was my girlfriend or something.

"I got caught up in some drama."

Finch kept looking at the car. "What's your name again?"

"Aaron."

"Well, Aaron. It's your lucky day. Remember what you asked for?"

"A jar."

"There's more, if you're interested."

Was he lying? Either way, I didn't trust him. Why should Finch make a special effort, especially after I flaked out on him?

He squinted. "Whose car is that?"

"My friend's older brother. So when can I pick it up?"

"Now," he said, turning back to the warehouse.

This was crazy. If I went inside, I could be stepping into a trap. I didn't even have a cell phone on me. I looked back at the car. This was my chance to redeem myself in front of the lead officer, not to mention lead him away from the girls. I doubted that I'd get another chance like this. Still, I must have hesitated.

"You sure about this?" Finch asked.

"I'm sure."

Another lie, maybe the biggest of all.

17 Carambola

Finch led me toward the back of the building. The rain had stopped and the road glistened like oil.

"Where are we headed?" I asked.

He didn't answer.

After we'd walked a few minutes, I asked, "Is it close?"

"Chill," Finch said. "We're here."

I saw nothing except an overgrown lot beside the train tracks. It would take a machete to hack through the thick jungle-like scrub.

"I'm not going in there," I said.

"God, you're making me paranoid. See that house?"

Then I spotted it, a stone cottage behind the vine-choked trees. The backyard was littered with rotten yellow fruit. I stepped over a husk swollen with flies.

"What is that? Mango?" I asked, remembering the rash on my feet.

Finch laughed. "You never ate starfruit before?" He grabbed a branch and shook it. The fruit toppled all around us, hitting the ground with a thunk. He took out a pocketknife and sawed into one lengthwise, showing me the star-shaped chunks. "The pioneers used to make wine from it," Finch said, popping a slice in his mouth. "Go on. Try."

I bit into it. The syrupy juice dribbled down my chin. "It's good," I mumbled.

On the front porch, a handmade sign read *Take off shoes.* So we did.

Finch kicked open the screen door. I followed behind. Who would've imagined that in the middle of this industrial wasteland, I would find starfruit, and now, a glassed-in room filled with more flower pots than I could count? They hung from the walls on S-shaped hooks. Others sat in wooden baskets on a picnic bench.

"This tiny one smells like dead meat," said Finch, tipping it toward me. "It's supposed to attract bugs."

"Where did they come from?" I asked, taking a sniff. He was right. It stank.

"My dad auctions them off. Some of these orchids are megarare. We steal them from the Everglades."

Talk about modern-day pirates.

"Really?" I said. "He sounds cool."

"You can meet him, he's right here," Finch said, stepping behind the picnic bench. There was a hulking, bare-chested man in a straw hat, misting plant roots with a spray bottle.

"Dad, this is Aaron," Finch said.

The man whipped off his hat. His broad skull was completely shaved.

"Call me Big Jack," he boomed in a voice full of twang. He tugged off his rubber gloves with his teeth. "You visiting Miami?" he asked, pronouncing it My-am-uh. "You're a god damned Yankee, eh?"

"Not exactly. I've traveled around a lot."

"That makes you a citizen of the world. Like me." He winked. "I bet you could use some Cuban coffee. Maybe a *cortadito*? I'm about to brew a pot."

"Actually, I've got to get back." I glanced at Finch, who was rocking on his heels.

"Won't take but a few minutes," his dad said, steering me into the kitchen.

I plunked myself down on a stool. Big Jack stood at the stove. He lit a match and the smell of gas flooded the room.

"The espresso maker is in that top left drawer," he told his son.

Finch rustled in a drawer and found a small metal pitcher.

"That's the one," said Big Jack. He took his time, scooping coffee grounds from a can of Bustelo.

I stared around the room. That's when I saw the guns mounted on the wall. Guns of all sizes, from Colt revolvers to shotguns to muskets, and even a few Civil War relics: long-barreled rifles and silver pistols with curlicues scraped into the handles.

"You collect antiques?" I asked, jabbing my thumb at the weapons.

Big Jack reached into the cabinet and pulled out a doll-sized cup. He dumped a couple tablespoons of sugar into it. "Those beauties? I inherited 'em," he said. "Did you know that Confederate soldiers used guns imported from England?"

"Really?" I said, as the blood pounded in my throat.

"What do they teach in school these days?" Big Jack asked. He poured a trickle into my cup and stirred.

"School blows," said Finch. "They just make you memorize the names and dates of battles and shit."

"That's right. It's all about death," Big Jack said. "Who died. When they died. Where they died." He blinked at me. "Go on. Bottoms up."

I took a sip. My tongue burned, but I knocked it back in one swallow.

"If you're so curious about the guns, let Finch take you outside. Test your luck with a little plinking," Big Jack said.

What the hell was he talking about? I was so busy thinking about death and guns, I didn't even notice that Finch had lifted a hunting rifle off the wall. He held it in both hands, like a gift.

"Let's fire up this bad boy," he said.

We shot at a trio of empty wine bottles, lined up on a log. After nailing each round, Finch poured black powder down the muzzle.

"If you don't load it the right way, it'll explode," he said.

I could barely hear, thanks to the wax plugs I'd screwed in my ears. Now it was my turn. Finch showed me how to lean the rifle on a rest (in this case, a musty sleeping bag). I pretended that I'd never done it before.

Finch said, "Don't hold it so tight. Keep your finger off the trigger until you're ready to fire."

I hunkered down on my belly, like I was about to blast a charging rhino. In the distance, I heard something clicking and whirring, almost like a lawn sprinkler.

"What's that noise?"

"Zombies," he said.

I pulled the trigger until it broke. A plume of white smoke puffed around us, but the bottles were untouched.

"Not bad," he said. "There's a crosswind blowing so we're going to move the target closer."

As he rearranged the bottles, I wondered if the cop was waiting for me back by the power plant, or if he'd issued an alert.

"Let's make a bet," I said, hoping this would speed things along.

"Yeah?" Finch said. "That's ballsy. One shot and you're making wages?"

"Why not? You go first, okay? Winner is the first to hit three in a row."

"Deal," he said. "Could do it in my sleep."

He reloaded. The rifle fired off another round of dust and noise. The bottle's skinny neck exploded and the bottom half wobbled off the log. He went again. This time, he missed. He didn't try for the third. Just passed the rifle to me.

"See if you can do better," he said.

I made the first shot, no problem. I was skewing my aim, preparing to miss, when Big Jack lumbered into the backyard.

"How's it going?" he asked, clapping a hand on his son's shoulder.

"It's Aaron's turn. He's good for a beginner," Finch said.

Big Jack cackled so hard, you could see metal glinting in his molars. "That boy? He don't look big enough to fit in my back pocket."

Stupid redneck. I took aim and the bottle toppled into pieces.

"Lucky shot," Big Jack said. "You got a talent for it. Would be a good thing, considering your size and all. Not like you'll ever take a man in a fistfight."

Before I realized it, I'd squeezed the trigger. The last bottle went down in a blink.

"Shit," said Finch. "You sure you've never done this before?"

His father nodded. "You did good, boy," he said, taking

the rifle from me. "Maybe you can join the army when you grow up."

"I'd rather be a cop," said Finch suddenly.

We locked eyes for a moment.

He laughed. "You know what? Being a cop would suck. Then I'd have to rat out all my friends."

"Whatever," I said, brushing off my greasy sneakers. "Don't change the subject," I told him, though that's exactly what I was doing. "I beat your ass, fair and square."

Finch gave a little shrug. "So what? You want a medal?"

I glanced around the backyard. I could still hear the clicking noises, like someone trying to crack open a safe. It was coming from a shed beyond the trees.

"What's in there?" I asked.

Big Jack was already walking away. "Don't you worry about that."

"Oh, what, is that where you hide your dead bodies?" I said, trying to make a joke.

Finch twitched his lips into a grin. "You really want to see?"

His father gave him a look. "That ain't your business."

"Actually, it is," said Finch, standing beside him.

They scowled at each other. The clicking noise grew louder, then stopped, as if I'd imagined it. Then I only heard cicadas sawing away in the oaks.

"Okay," said Big Jack. "The boy earned it."

We walked to the shed. Big Jack was still holding the gun. The shed looked like a vacation cottage for the seven dwarves: a tiled roof and a window trimmed with an empty flowerbox and shutters that were nailed closed.

Finch reached into the flowerbox and pulled out a key. My grandma used the same trick when she was stuck in the hospital one summer and I babysat her Siamese cats. Finch jiggled the lock and the door creaked open.

The smell was the first thing that hit me: thick and tangy, like rotting carpet. "This is some operation, you've got here," I said, as Finch showed off the high-powered lamps, the whirring fans, the automatic watering system hitched to the ceiling, not to mention the thousands of dollars worth of marijuana plants.

"Lay your eyes on this. Been growing about eight weeks." He pinched a leaf dusted with yellowy pollen.

"That's all you got?"

Finch glared. "Who's doing business with you? Nobody's got better quality than this," he said. "You buying dime bags from Morgan?"

"Maybe," I said.

"And where do you think she gets it? Take a guess. She ain't growing that shit in her daddy's backyard."

"What about the jar?"

"Hey, man. You didn't show. I had to sell it."

"What? Then why did you bring me here?"

"I thought you'd be interested in this," he said.

Big Jack cut between us. "How about we go inside?"

"Okay," I said.

Big Jack slung his arm around me. In the other, he held the rifle.

"Good answer."

18 Rolling

Big Jack gave me a bag of something called ahahuasca. He said it came from the rain forest.

"Don't smoke it," he said.

"Why not?"

"That would insult the goddess," he said, tapping his forehead, as if the goddess lived in there. "And you don't want to make her angry."

We shook hands. Then the door creaked shut, and I was back outside, wondering what the hell just happened.

I asked Finch, "Is your dad for real?"

Finch ripped a stalk of tall grass. He shoved it in his mouth and chewed. "Don't knock my old man. He used to live in the jungle. He's seen all kinds of crazy shit."

"What the hell am I supposed to do with this?" I asked, dangling the baggie.

"Boil it on the stove."

"Then what?"

He smirked. "Drink up."

"You tried it?"

"Sure," he said. I couldn't tell if he was lying.

"How many times?"

"*Mucho*," he said.

"So what happens when you take it?"

He spat on the ground. "Geez, you're full of questions. Look. It changes your view of reality. Nothing is what it seems on the surface, you know? People wear masks. This strips everything down to its elemental level. It reveals truths, you know?"

"Sure." I nodded.

Finch kept rambling. Nothing I hadn't heard before. All this New Agey talk was grating my nerves.

"So your dad goes to the Everglades a lot?" I asked.

"That's where he gets the orchids." Finch squatted on the sidewalk and took a Philly Blunt from his shirt pocket. He tore it open and dumped out the tobacco.

"Ever heard of people throwing parties over there?"

"You mean like raves?" Finch said with a hint of sarcasm. He spun his fists, as if glowsticking. "Is that what you're looking for?"

"I dunno. It's stupid, I guess."

Finch produced a little baggie of weed and spread it into the blunt wrap. He licked the edge, like he was mailing a letter. "I heard there's a party coming up on Halloween."

"Yeah, I saw something about it online," I said, wondering how much Finch knew.

"Could be wack," he said. "Or the sickest event of all time." He flicked his lighter across the blunt, sealing it dry.

"You going?"

"Maybe." Finch sparked it up, then sucked in a lungful of smoke. He passed it to me. I pinched it between my fingers, as if it were alive. Strong stuff. Finch watched me gulp and cough. "You got asthma or something?" he said, laughing. He snatched the blunt and took another long toke. Smoke dribbled out of his nose. Now it was my turn again. We passed it back and forth.

Finch reached into his pocket. "Hold that thought." He pulled out his cell phone and squinted at it. "My dad's giving me grief. You know your way back, right?"

"I think so."

"Cool. I'll catch you later."

He walked toward the house.

As I crossed the backyard, stepping over bruised and swollen starfruit, I saw something glinting behind the trees. I waited until Finch had disappeared inside, then snuck a closer look. Buried in the weeds was an airboat. It was about twelve feet long and rigged with a caged propeller so large, it looked like it could fly as well as cruise through a swamp. No doubt, that's how Big Jack transported his stolen orchids from the Everglades.

I traced my finger in the mud smeared across the seat. As a kid, I used to climb on a broken-down Jeep I found disintegrating in the lot behind my grandmother's house. I'd pretend it was a pirate ship, sailing to buried treasure.

I'd always had a knack for pretending. Now it was getting harder to remember which part of myself I'd disguised. Which parts were real? And which were fake?

I gawked at the airboat. It was tangled in the sawgrass like those hidden pictures in the magazines I they had at the orthodontist's office. Find the bunny in the tree branches or clouds. My eyes scanned the license plate: H10FCR.

It was one of those stupid vanity plates that never made sense, no matter how you said it. I sounded out the letters until something clicked. Hi, officer. A smartass salute to a cop. I walked faster. Where had I seen that before? It might've been the weed or the Cuban coffee or whatever, but I couldn't help looking over my shoulder every two seconds as I walked. Even the warehouse, with its chain link fence and barbed wire, seemed to ripple and snap, ever so slowly, like a sail.

The lead officer was waiting in the car. By now, the light had melted into a dim purplish glow, but he never took off his shades. I was still thinking about the vanity plate when the lead officer cracked the window and said, "Where the hell have you been?"

He didn't change his expression when I showed him the plastic baggie.

"You've been gone for over two hours," he said, "and you come back with a bag of tea leaves?"

"You should've seen all their guns. It was like a war museum."

He sniffed the baggie. "What's this stuff called again?"

"Ahahuasca. It's from Brazil."

"Never heard of it."

I fiddled with a loose thread on my shirt hem. Once again, I felt like I'd let him down. "His dad gave it to me."

"So there was no transaction involved with the dealer?"

"I guess you could say that."

"Why do you think he's our alpha dog?" he asked.

"Oh, he is. I'm sure about it."

"What makes you believe that?"

"Well, for one thing, he's growing thousands of dollars worth of marijuana in his back shed."

"How do you know he's supplying it to the school?"

Finch had said he dealt it to Morgan, who was doing business at Skully's party. But I couldn't bring myself to say their names. Instead I mumbled:

"He was selling at the warehouse the other night."

"You witnessed this guy offering narcotics to his friends, but you're not even sure if it was cocaine or ketamine. Now he gives you this stuff for free. That doesn't make him the shot caller." He tucked the bag in his pocket. "I'll take it down to the station and run a test on it."

For some reason, when I heard "run a test," I pictured the cop lighting up, although Big Jack said it would insult the goddess. The whole scene played out in my head like a cartoon, and I snickered.

"Think this is funny?" he asked, leaning so close, I wondered if he could smell the smoke on my clothes.

"No, sir."

"This was a mistake," he said, rubbing his temples. "I told them you were too young."

I tugged at my sock.

"Look," he said. "I think you're losing sight of what's important. These kids are not your buddies. Got it?"

"Yes, sir."

"Think of it this way. If they found out the truth, that you're a snitch, they would make sure you paid for it. I guarantee it."

We drove around the block. The officer was rambling about my broken cell phone, but I wasn't paying attention. "Hopefully we can get it fixed without losing all those phone numbers you've acquired."

"They're stored on the SIM card," I said. That's when I made the connection with the vanity plate. I'd seen the same letters online. It was that guy's screen name, the one who sent the invite to the Glades Party, as the girls kept calling it. Was Finch the one behind it? And did he hack into my account and create that fake profile?

"There's something else I need to tell you," I said, breaking the silence.

"What's that?"

"There's a major party coming up on Halloween. It's in the Everglades. All the players are going to show."

"You better be talking about the entire school here," he said. "Because if we send in the foot soldiers and this turns out to be a waste of time, we'll have to call off the entire operation. Understand?"

"Yes, sir."

He slowed for a stoplight. When it turned green, he hit the gas. A boy on a bicycle sped through the intersection. The cop jerked the wheel, and I slammed against the glove box. The boy didn't even look up. He just kept pedaling.

"Oh, my god." I whistled through my teeth.

"Yeah. Exactly," he muttered. "That kid must have a guardian angel looking out for him somewheres."

"Or a devil," I added.

"What makes you say that?"

"Because he's riding my bike."

———

Status: UNSENT
To: LadyM
From: Metroid
Subject: 21st Century Breakdown

Dear Morgan,

I'm in Study Skills class in the library and I'm so freaking bored. I can't even close my eyes. It's like I've become one with my desk. The librarian is really young (wannabe adult). I had him last year. He always talks about his perfect life and hands out pictures of himself, his wedding, his baby, etc. But do I really mind him getting off the subject?

There is music coming from the computer lab upstairs (Stanky Legg) and people are laughing. God, they're so easily entertained. Now a group of freshman girls just walked by and said, "Ohhhh. You type so fast." That was random. Some of the girls in this school look 40 and some of them look 12. Don't think I'm a pervert or whatever. Just something I've noticed.

This guy is really into being a teacher. The worst thing about this class is Vocab. I was going to change my schedule and he was like, "Do your best while you're in here." I might try harder if I actually cared. I mean, they should teach us something useful, like how to balance your checkbook. But I guess there's computer programs for that.

How many times can I type the word BORING? Right now, Skully is saying (like she's happy) "I got all Cs on my report card," like she doesn't have the mental capacity to do better. Not that I should talk. On my last quiz, I got an

F-. (What the hell is the minus for? Another jab at my decaying self-esteem?)

Here's what I think. Skully pretends to be stupid because she wants people to like her. You would think she's got it made—bigass house, a car that costs more than what my mom makes in a year, etc. But nobody seems to actually care about her. Today at lunch, she came out of the bathroom and it looked like she'd been crying. I think she hides in there. That's what I used to do, like, constantly, last year.

It feels like everybody is watching and waiting for you to fail.

One time, I sneezed during a test. This kid turned around and told me to shut up, like I had broken his concentration on purpose. I was hella pissed, but I didn't do shit about it.

We're living in a war zone. Obviously, it's not the hardcore stuff my dad saw in the Middle East. I can't even imagine that. Believe me, I've tried.

As I've already mentioned before... I'm a total coward.

When I was a kid, I spent hours doodling epic space battles. (I'll spare you the details). I had this whole universe inside my head: humans vs. aliens. Typical, right? Except the way I drew it, the aliens were heroes.

Back then, it was so much easier, separating the good guys from the bad.

I'm still working on my plan to keep you safe.

The last time we talked (in person), lunch had just ended. I gave you a piggyback ride up the stairs. You made a big deal about it, like I was Mr. Strongman or whatever. When you kissed me on the roof the other day, it was so amazing. I can't stop thinking about that.

I keep wishing I could go back in time and start over. Maybe in an alternate dimension, I wouldn't run that red light. The cop wouldn't pull me over. I wouldn't be in this mess.

But maybe I wouldn't have met you.

—A.

19 Digging

When I got home, the first thing I noticed was the truck. Somebody had slashed all the tires. The windshield was broken. Bullets of glass sparkled in the back seat. But that's not what freaked me the most. There, dripping across both doors, were spray-painted letters in all caps:

DIE NARC SCUM

The words burned into my retinas. I felt like throwing up. For some reason, I started pacing on the sidewalk. I was scared to get near the truck, like there might be ninjas lurking in the trunk. Or dead bodies.

Okay. *Calm the fuck down*, I told myself. Whoever did the damage was gone, obviously. But they'd be back. Oh, God. What if they hurt Haylie? I ran upstairs, shoved my key in the lock and flung open the door. Mom had torn the place apart. She'd stripped the curtains off the window, letting in the late afternoon sunlight, which coated the room like a varnish. Only a few trampled feathers were left on the windowsill, along with a bone-white egg. How long had it been there? Maybe it never hatched? It rested alone, abandoned, like a fossil.

On top of the Murphy bed, I found some of my old junk—a stack of memo pads, my World History book, and a few of Dad's cast-offs, including a pirate coffee mug decorated with leg bones.

"If you see anything you want, just holler. Otherwise I'm tossing it," Mom said.

How could she just throw Dad's stuff away?

I squinted up at her, shielding the light with my fist. "Mom, I've got something to tell you. I'm taking off for a little while."

"What do you mean, 'taking off'? You have school. And who's going to watch Haylie when I'm at work?"

I couldn't tell her the truth: Haylie was the reason I had to leave.

I was marching back and forth like a robot. "I need some space to myself. This place is too small. Besides. Haylie's a smart kid. She can take care of herself. Most of the time, she's not even home."

"Yeah. That's what concerns me," Mom said. "Some kid called here, looking for her last night."

"What kid?"

"Actually, I shouldn't say 'kid' because he sounded a lot older."

My chest crumpled. "Was it her boyfriend?"

Mom unrolled a foot of masking tape, stretched it across one of the boxes, marked *Kitchen,* and tore it off with her teeth. "I must be going deaf. Because for a minute, I thought I heard the b-word: *boyfriend.*"

I stopped pacing. I'd lied to everyone, but I couldn't lie to my mom.

"You heard right," I said.

"Well, she's way too young to be dating. Do you know this boy?"

"I have no clue who he is. Where's Haylie now?"

"At a friend's house."

"What else is new?" I muttered. "Shit."

"Watch your mouth," Mom said. "I'm getting sick and tired of your attitude, mister."

"Have you seen the truck?"

"Well, it's probably in the parking lot where I left it. Been meaning to get the brakes redone, but we can't afford it right now."

Mom was so out of it, she hadn't even seen the vandalism. When did it take place? Last night? Or this afternoon? Did they really have the balls to do something like that in broad daylight? What else were they going to do? I wasn't sticking around to find out.

"Aaron." Mom set the box aside. "Feel like talking?"

I did.

But I couldn't.

I'd dug a hole so deep, there was only one thing left to do:

Dig deeper.

I walked fifteen blocks in the dark to a coffee shop with free Wi-Fi. Unzipped my bag and took out my laptop. The hundred-year-old waitress kept scurrying over to my booth, trying to get me to order more coffee and pastelitos, which are greasy pastries stuffed with ground meat. When I logged onto Facebook and checked my page, Morgan had left a comment:

> Yo Mr. Crunk,
> Call me 2night.
> I've got interesting badness/madness stories for you.
> <3333333333

I dialed her number on the pay phone. No answer. Next, I tried e-mailing:

> Are you online? Hit me with an IM.

Minutes later, she still hadn't responded. I plunked another coin in the slot. Who else could I call? Skully didn't pick up. Morgan said Skully always let her batteries die. Then she'd forget to recharge them. I thought about calling Morgan at home, but I imagined her stepmom on the other end, screening me out. Finally, I punched the numbers. It rang twice, then Sheryl's voice bellowed in my ear.

"Are you that man?" she said. No *hello* or *how are you.* That was weird.

There was a clatter, then a strangled noise, as if she'd choked the phone down her throat. Footsteps pounded. A dog yapped three times. I waited for Sheryl to come back, but she didn't, so I gave up.

I dipped back inside and rested my forehead on the table. The waitress mumbled at me from far away.

"You all right, baby? You need anything?"

"Another cortadito," I said without lifting my head. "*Por favor.*"

Since my gun-shooting adventure with Finch, I'd become addicted to the stuff. I knocked back another doll-sized cup and my hands trembled. Dad used to guzzle coffee all day like a fiend. "Just hook me to an IV and pump the caffeine into my veins," he'd joke.

When Dad used to send an e-mail, I'd have to wade through all this us.airforce.mil blabber at the top before I got to his letters: CLASSIFICATION: UNCLASSIFIED. Usually, it was a picture of a freeze-dried dinner, what Dad called MRE (meals ready to eat) or SOS (shit on a shingle) complete with Photoshopped arrows pointing around his plate.

This is Menu Number Nineteen, he'd write. *Pot roast with vegetables.*

Dad even took pictures of the packages, which featured

a cartoon of a gun-toting soldier at the top beside the "resealable seal."

He never sent the kind of photos that landed him on the front pages of magazines. He never told me about the "conflict in the Mideast," as they called it on TV. He told me about gross food. And the weather.

I knew it was Dad's job to stay neutral. I just wished the man had opened up every once in a while.

Mom always said that I looked exactly like him. She was wrong. I didn't look anything like Dad.

He was supposed to protect us. He was supposed to take care of his family. Liar.

Maybe I was more like him than I thought.

I called Skully again. This time, she answered.

"Hey, Double A," she said. "I can't talk long. My *abuela* is yelling at me to watch TV with her."

"Oh. Right." My voice cracked. I sounded like an idiot.

"Yeah. She's really cool. We watch all those variety shows on Univision, you know? Like, on Saturday we watch *Sabado Gigante* and she'll say, 'Ay. Those women need to put their clothes on.' But if I turn the channel, she'll throw pillows at me."

"Skully, I'm in deep shit."

For once, she stopped talking. Here goes.

"My mom kicked me out of the apartment."

"Oh, my god. What happened?"

"She started freaking out, you know? Hitting me and stuff. She drinks too much. You saw how crazy she is."

"Yeah, she did seem a little crazy. Did she hurt you really bad?"

"Nah, I'm fine. I just need a place to stay."

"You can crash here," Skully said. "Everybody does."

"When can I come over?"

"Whenever. I'm up all night."

"One more thing," I added.

"What's that?"

"I don't have a ride."

"Your truck's busted? That sucks. Look. I'll be there in an hour. Get your stuff together and wait outside. What's the address again?"

I gave her the directions.

"Got it. Be safe, okay? I'll see you in a bit," she said.

By the time I walked back to the apartment and stopped at an ATM for cash, I only had a few minutes to throw a few jeans and T-shirts into a duffel, along with clean boxers, an extra pair of sneakers, Morgan's crumpled self-portrait, my school stuff, and a toothbrush.

When I came outside, Haylie was sitting on the front step.

"You made Mom cry," she said, and I felt like scum, just like the spray painted words on the truck said I was. "Why are you ditching us?"

I wanted to explain everything. I wanted Haylie to know that I was leaving to keep our family safe. Instead, I asked, "Who's the guy that called last night? Was he your friend?" I cringed, thinking of the lead officer's term for me.

"Oh, my god. You told Mom, didn't you?" Her eyes were red-rimmed and sleepy. She was wearing lip-gloss. Her mouth looked like a bruise.

"Since when did you start using makeup? I just want to know—"

"You ratted me out." Haylie sobbed so hard, she began to hiccup. "Just go. I don't want you here. I wish you were dead instead of Dad."

"Me too," I said. And that was the truth.

Haylie stomped back inside the apartment. I didn't even get to hug her goodbye. Skully pulled up within seconds, driving a silver Hummer. I piled everything in the back.

"That's all the stuff you brought?" she asked. "Geez. I bring more suitcases when we go to Disney World."

I jumped in the front seat. Skully spun the car around, knocking over the garbage can as we back out.

"Whoops," she said. "That's what bumpers are for." She glanced up at the apartment building. "Isn't that your mom?"

In the window, Mom watched us leave. She was clutching a beer and her face had tightened into a frown.

"You're right," said Skully. "She really is crazy. But she seemed nice."

"She is."

Skully stared.

"I mean, she's a mixture of both," I said.

"Right," Skully said. "Isn't everybody?"

"That's the truth."

And I meant it. Every word.

Dear Morgan,

This morning, I was at the Spirit Shop and Brent was behind me, talking shit about you. For real. You should stay away from him. No joke. He's a tool. One time, he stole a Coke from this seventh grader and threw it out the window. And today he had a little freakout in Art. How is that even possible? It's, like, the easiest class in the universe. You paint a horse or a flower or whatever and Mrs. Garber gives you an A and writes, "Good!" on the back. (I bet she puts the same thing on everybody's papers, it's probly a stamp or something).

Anyway.

Brent got mad for some unknown reason. He started throwing paint at Nolan Struth. Then he shoved his desk across the room. Mrs. Garber actually looked scared. She gave Brent a lunch detention and he tore it up.

That kid has serious anger management issues. Did you really go out with him? It makes me want to puke, just thinking about it.

I hate when people slam their books on the table. I'm in the library, trying to type this stupid e-mail, but my mind is a TV that keeps changing channels. You're probably in Geometry right now. You're in the second row, third seat from the left (Is it just me or do you always sit in the same spot?). You're wearing that awesome dress with the butterfly buttons again and your hair smells really good, like a forest or something.

I'm totally creeping you out, right?

Last year, I used to hide in the library. Pretty lame, I know. (Not to mention, totally unoriginal). I wasted so much time, reading weird stuff on the Internet. I remember this moment exactly, the day I learned about string theory. Maybe you've heard of it? Scientists believe that every choice we make...it's like, already been done in some other dimension. This basically means that we have no free will. Everything that could happen has already happened.

I keep trying to wrap my head around it. (Ever try to imagine infinity? It looks like a bunch of zeros that go on forever). If string theory is real, there's another dimension where assholes like Brent don't exist. And I'm just Aaron Foster, not Informant Number blah blah blah. And this entire year hasn't even started yet. It's a clean slate. "Tabula rasa," as Aristotle would say.

I want to zap myself into another dimension.

—A.

20 Big Cheese

Soon I was hanging with Skully and Morgan every weekend. This is what I should've done last year instead of playing Halo3 on the Xbox and stalking girls in chatrooms.

Skully took good care of her guests. She brought her little brother orange juice in the morning, which she squished with her bare hands into a soup bowl. Sebastian went to some Catholic junior high school where they memorized Bible quotes for homework. Their grandmother watched TV all day in the "maid's quarters" (although I'd never seen a maid there), and a stream of nameless people flowed in and out of the garage at all hours.

I was sleeping on a pullout bed that unfolded from a leather couch upstairs. Each morning, I shaved with Skully's pink plastic razor, which she used to sculpt the back of her neck.

She told me to lose the goatee.

"You look more like yourself without it," she said.

I lathered up and scraped it off. My chin itched all day. When Morgan saw me at school, she said, "I'm glad you finally nixed the soul patch," and I couldn't stop smiling.

Me and Skully were always late to school. For the next few weeks, we sleepwalked through class until she drove us back to the McMansion. It sure beat living on crappy Biscayne Boulevard. On Fridays, we met up with Morgan (unless she was grounded) and read magazines and drank bottomless frappuccinos at the bookstore, and made fun of the coffee dude, who always threatened to throw us out and never did.

Just when I'd started to forget about this Halloween business, one of the girls would mention it again. The party was coming up in a couple of days. They called it a "birthday blowout" for Morgan. Since she was turning eighteen, they were making a big deal about it. Morgan spilled the news to Brent, who wasn't exactly thrilled that his ex-girlfriend heard about the party from me.

The cops hadn't forgotten either.

I met my "friend" one last time in a rented storage room, not far from the expressway. There was nothing in the place. Just a bare bulb flickering in the ceiling. I leaned against the wall while the cop paced. He seemed more agitated than usual.

"Take this," he said, handing over my cell, which looked just like new. "When you get to the location, you will send a text message. No phone calls. Understand? This will be the 'take down' signal. And the phone signal is how we'll find you."

He rambled on about "showtime" and "cranking up the ante." When I told him about my truck and the DIE NARC SCUM message, he didn't seem to care.

"You signed that paper," he said, meaning the substantial assistance agreement. "We treated you like an adult. Now you have to act like one."

More than anything, I just wanted to run away. Tell my mom the truth. I mean, they made me sign without her permission. But even that wasn't completely true. I signed that damn paper, all on my own.

"Once the signal is given," he went on, "you need to remove yourself from the situation."

"You mean ... ditch everyone?"

"Unless you want to go to jail, yeah. Nobody's going to be looking out for you. Got it?"

I explained about crashing at Skully's place and he said, "Smart move." I finally felt like I was doing something right. At the same time, I wasn't completely convinced.

"This makes it safer for my family, right?" I asked.

He grunted. "Like I said before, I can't make any promises. Until we catch this guy, there's always a chance that someone will get hurt. You. Your family. The kids at the school. Nobody is safe."

"And if we don't catch him?"

"Someone will get hurt. I guarantee it. Now it's up to you. Make sure all the players show."

"Okay, okay," I told him. God. Would he ever get off my back?

"We've done our part. Now you need to do yours."

I thought about my dad's truck, the words spray-painted like blood. Mom blamed it on our shitty neighborhood. Did she even know what *narc* meant?

I had the feeling I was just beginning to learn.

———

On the day before Morgan's birthday, I couldn't concentrate in class. As I flipped through the pages in my World Civilization book, I found doodles in number two pencil.

The Greeks=sexist assholes, somebody wrote in Bubblicious handwriting.

I couldn't help wondering who scribbled in my book, years before I came to this school. Who were they to judge? The Greeks lived a long time ago; they didn't know any better. Or maybe they knew more.

Turning a chapter ahead, I found more comments in the margins: *WTF? Kill me now. I can't take any more of this torture…*

What was so important that this person couldn't sit at a desk for forty-five minutes and listen to a few ancient stories? I could think of a lot worse places to be.

On the next page, they wrote:

How old is Mr. Pitstick?
a. 40
b. 50
c. 60
d. All of the above, added together.

I busted out a laugh. A girl in the front row turned around. She was sort of cute, despite the constellation of pimples dotting her chin. I turned back to my book and pretended to read. After skimming the same paragraph five times in a row, I realized that I had absorbed nothing. God, I was so out of it.

My phone vibrated inside my bag, making a noise like a dying muffler. Mr. Pitstick got so frazzled, he dropped his marker.

"Whose phone is that?" he called out.

"Sorry," I told him. "I just got it fixed and I forgot to turn it off."

"Well, do that," he said.

The bell rang a few moments later, and everybody grabbed their stuff. Mr. Pitstick yelled, "Stay in your seats. You've got an essay due on Monday. Listen up, people." A communal groan washed across the classroom.

Later I caught up with Skully in the parking lot. Morgan was there, smothered under her headphones. The girls leaned against the dented Explorer, laughing as they shared a cigarette. Looking at them, a spreadsheet unfolded in my head—punk, emo, Goth—but I couldn't make sense of these labels anymore. I called them the Muses, like the sister-goddesses in Greek mythology.

Morgan flicked the cigarette onto the pavement. I watched it smolder and fizzle, the smoke rising like slow-motion calligraphy.

"Hey, hey, hey," she said in her wispy voice.

"What do I look like? A horse?" I said, faking a smile.

She smirked. "Yeah. Actually, you do," she said, kissing my cheek. "What's up, rocker?"

I leaned in to return the kiss, the standard Miami greeting, but I moved right instead of left, causing a brief collision. I ended up smooching her thick bangs, which smelled like health-store shampoo—rosemary and mint.

Skully snatched my hand and planted a big wet one on it. "How's it going, Double A? No sugar for me? Don't you love me anymore?"

I wrapped her into a hug. "Of course I do."

The girls wouldn't stop talking about the Glades party.

"My costume is going to be so amazing," said Morgan.

All I wanted to do is get behind the wheel and drive, take the girls with me, as far north as 95 will carry us, to a place far away, where the leaves had changed color.

"You can't be serious about this party," I told them.

"Oh, we're dead serious," says Skully, cackling like a mad scientist.

"Dressing up was always my favorite part about Halloween," Morgan said. "I could've cared less about the candy. Except for the Hershey bars. Or the Butterfingers."

"I always put those in the fridge. They taste better frozen," said Skully. "Did you go trick-or-treating when you were little?" she asked me.

"A couple times. I don't really remember."

"He's lying," said Morgan. "What are you trying to hide? Did your mom make you wear a pillowcase with holes cut into it?"

"Actually, yes," I said. "But that didn't suck as much as the actual trick-or-treating. See, we were living in an apartment on base. And there were like, no other little kids around. So we got in the elevator and knocked on people's doors. They weren't prepared or anything. All I got was an apple and some old man candy."

"Gross. What's that?"

"You know. Those chalky mints you get with the bill in Italian restaurants."

"Oh, that's tragic. We have to make up for lost time," she said, patting my head. "You're going, even if I have to tie you up and drag you there."

"Thanks."

"We'll even help you pick out a costume," said Skully.

"He'd look good in a mask," said Morgan. She talked about me in the third person, as if I didn't exist. I realized they did that a lot. "He should go as a superhero or something."

"A superhero in tights," Skully added.

"Hm," said Morgan. "It's my birthday, right? All I'm saying is … I better get lots of presents."

"Oh, you will. You invited the entire school. Except Danica Stone, who will probably find out anyway. That skank."

"You invited more people? How?" I asked.

"Online. Duh," said Skully. "It's going to be so amazing. And it's in the middle of nowhere. So who the hell is going to stop us?"

"Enough talking. Let's get out of here," said Morgan.

I opened the car door and climbed in the front. Cranked the radio, just to smother the noise inside my head. All the songs about hearts and dreams and tears didn't do any good.

"It's freaking hot in here," said Morgan, switching on a portable fan duct-taped to the dashboard. Her driving skills hadn't improved. The Explorer groaned and sputtered and finally stalled in the middle of the highway.

"You're going to wear out the clutch," I told her.

"Fine. Since you're the expert, you can drive."

She threw the keys in my lap. I had no choice except to slide behind the wheel.

The girls screeched at me to drive faster, so I hit the gas. I had to admit, this was a hell of a lot more exciting than driving my dad's old truck. I was perched so high, I could peer into the smaller sedans beside us, see people messing with their cell phones or munching fries. One woman was actually painting her nails, right on top of the steering wheel.

Morgan rattled off directions. She kind of sounded

like her stepmom. "Turn right here. No, I mean left. That's right."

I veered into a barren strip mall. There was a military Jeep parked beside an Army Surplus store, and a mannequin draped in fatigues. We got out and the sun drilled into my eyes. As we breezed through the door, a chain of cowbells jingled and slammed against the handle, startling me out of my head.

Skully called, "Hey, Alvaro!" to the dude behind the cash register.

He nodded, and they talked a million miles per hour in Spanish.

"I hate when she does that," Morgan said, drifting into the guns and ammo aisle. She picked up a pair of aviator goggles and slid them over her face. "Bang," she said, cocking her finger. "You're dead."

"Do you really hate me that much?"

She pushed the goggles against her forehead, making it seem like she had grown another set of eyes. "Don't flatter yourself, player."

"Look. I don't think I'm a player or anything. I'm sorry those rumors about us got spread around. But trust me, I'm not the one who did it."

"I know," she said.

"How do you know?"

"Because you're a nice person."

I held my breath. "What makes you say that?"

"I'm a really good judge of character."

"Right. You can't pull the wool over your ice," I said.

Morgan smirked. "You're weird," she said, ruffling my hair. She grabbed my hand and tugged. I squeezed her fingers, which always seemed cold. "Help me pick out something that doesn't suck," she said, squeezing back.

The guy behind the counter said, "Look at Romeo here, surrounded by two beautiful girls. What's your secret? Just be yourself, yeah? That's what they say on TV. But it's bull. Nobody gets laid by being themselves."

"Stop corrupting him," Skully said. "Aaron is a pure spirit."

Morgan snorted. "There is no such thing."

"I can pretend, right?" Skully shouted, turning the heads of a few people at the register.

Afterwards, we drove to the Big Cheese, a South Miami pizza place. It was packed with college people and screaming kids. Skully's little brother, Sebastian, was already waiting at the table.

"It took me like, a half hour to skate here," he said. "Now I've got muscles on top of my muscles."

I slid between the girls. They shouted over my head like a pair of stereo speakers. They were squawking so loudly that the people in the next booth told us to "tone it down."

Sebastian took out a plastic Circle K bag and tried to unwrap something inside it, but Skully caught him.

"No candy."

"I'm not doing anything," he said.

"I can hear the wrapper crinkling. You know better."

Skully handed him a fun-sized diabetic granola bar from her bag. "Eat this and shut up."

"This would be better if it had chocolate chips. You know, I would eat myself if I were chocolate," he said with his mouth full.

"Then you'd be dead."

I took another swig of the flat Coke that Skully bought for me. She always paid for everything on her debit card. Yet another reason to feel like a complete asshole.

"You remind me of the long-haired dude in that surfer movie," Sebastian said.

"Is that a good thing?"

Skully glanced around the table. "He does, right? Look. He's turning red."

Just hearing the phrase, "He's turning red," took me back to the cafeteria in seventh grade. I listened to the girls laughing, and I got nervous all over again, staring into the grease stains on my paper plate. Maybe hanging with girls had its drawbacks.

"My homeroom teacher is a girl," said Sebastian, "which is good because the boy teachers are mean. But she always gets my name wrong. I'm like, you're a teacher. Sound it out," he said. "But it's okay. I like older women."

"Good for you!" Morgan thumped the table. Then she moved onto another topic: My ex-girlfriend.

"Was your ex pretty?" she wanted to know.

"Can we talk about something else?" I asked. Having an ex was another lie I told to fit in.

"Look at his face. He's still in love with her," Skully said.

I studied my napkin.

Later, the girls filed into the bathroom, as if they were having a conference in there. Who knows? Maybe they were.

Skully's brother stayed behind, and we headed for the car after I finished my flat, watered-down Coke. As we walked through the deserted parking lot, he said, "I think Morgan is into you."

This is how low I'd stooped. I was getting advice from a thirteen-year-old.

"We're just friends," I said.

It was true. Why would a cool girl like Morgan be interested in me? I might catch her eye for a while, but it was all fake, so it wouldn't last long. She'd get bored. This was exactly where I always got stuck, doomed to the friend zone. My sister would probably have an opinion about it... like she did about everything. I never thought I would miss her so much. Or Mom, who started crying every time I called now. So I just stopped calling.

I pulled out my cell and sent Haylie a text message:
OLA KALA?

Minutes passed. Nice. Haylie was ignoring me, just like Collin as soon as he escaped to his fancy college.

I was shivering as I walked to the car. Skully was already in the driver's seat, honking the horn. I took my time. The night air felt cooler than I could remember, and it was beginning to rain. But it was a good kind of cold. It let me know I was still alive.

"Aaron. Wait up."

I turned. There was Morgan, clip-clopping after me in her wooden flip-flops. She stopped in the middle of the parking lot, kicked them off, and carried them in both hands.

Then she gave me a hug—a genuine embrace, not one of those fake half ones. I felt like there was more to say, but never enough time. Or it was never the right time.

I looked at her bare feet, at her painted toenails.

"Hop in," I said, opening the door.

Morgan slid next to me in the backseat. Her knees bumped against mine. Neither of us said anything.

In the passenger seat up front, Sebastian twisted around. "No funny business."

"Shut up," his sister said.

Driving along US-1, Skully rolled down the window. I dangled my hand until the tips of my fingers turned numb. Nothing to hear except the tires rolling forward and a deep, still quiet of the air rushing by.

I leaned back and listened.

21 Fumble

As we pulled up to Skully's house, all the lights winked out. The rain had picked up speed, and it looked like the entire neighborhood had lost electricity, judging by the curtain of blackness around the block.

"How long before the power comes back?" I asked.

Skully hunted for her keys, dripping and swearing. "Damn it. I can't even find the door knob."

Only a month ago, Morgan was showing me around the house. Now I was clutching her damp hand and pulling her into the living room. We bumped into chairs and stumbled over the carpet. Rain drummed the roof, never slowing.

Everyone went to Skully's room to watch a movie on her laptop, but Morgan said she didn't feel like it.

"I'm all sweaty," she said.

I had already peeled off my T-shirt. The house was sweltering without the AC. Plus it was so quiet, I could hear my heart thudding away.

"I've got an idea," Morgan told me. "Let's go swimming."

"In a rainstorm?"

"It's not like it's thundering or anything. Come on, you wuss. Are you scared?"

"No," I said. It wasn't the rain that was making me nervous.

"You are totally scared! I can tell," she said.

Morgan squealed and ran down the stairs. I followed after her. When we reached the patio door, she flung it open. Both of us stood in the rain, completely soaked. Morgan stuck out her tongue, as if catching snowflakes. I wondered if she'd ever seen snow.

I watched, dumbfounded, as she tugged off her blouse. It was dark, but I could see her milk-white skin, which almost seemed to glow. She began to wiggle out of her jeans.

"It's weird if you watch me do this," she said.

"What do you want me to do?"

"Turn around. And no peeking."

"I'm not."

At last, she said, "Okay, I'm ready."

She was just in a bra and panties, which isn't that different from a bikini. Yet somehow, it is. Her thighs were etched with tiny scars. It hurt to look at them.

"Now you," she said.

Morgan watched me unbuckle my pants and drop them to the ground. I kicked them across the patio.

"That was dramatic," she said.

She laced her fingers through mine. We took off, jogging toward the deep end. At the last minute, she let go. I plunged in, feet-first, and sank to the bottom, where I looked up at the raindrops dotting the surface of the pool like Braille. Then I paddled my way to the ladder and pulled myself out.

"Shit," I said.

"What's up?" Morgan asked.

"I lost one of my contacts." No use keeping the other one, so I pinched it out, too.

"I didn't know you wore contacts," she said. "You should just get Lasik or something."

"A laser beam in my eye? No thanks," I said, blinking at the trees. At least, they looked like trees. "Why aren't you jumping in? You tricked me," I told Morgan.

She giggled. "What are you going to do about it?"

"This," I said, lunging toward her. She ran, but I was too fast. I locked my arms around her waist and we fell backward into the water. Morgan flailed against me, scissoring her legs. We rose up, sputtering. Her hair was plastered against her face. I smoothed it away and kissed her lips, tasting salt. My hands slid over her thighs. Morgan pulled away. She swam to the edge and clung there, never taking her eyes off me.

"You're evil," she said, gasping.

I stood near the pool steps, the rain spilling on me. I had no idea what to say to this girl.

"I told you not to watch me," she said.

"What am I supposed to look at? You're the one who wanted to go swimming."

"I know," she said, lowering her head. That's when I figured it out.

"Are you afraid that I'm going to see your scars?" I asked.

Morgan nodded. A surge of guilt washed over me.

"Well, I can't see much of anything right now. And besides, I don't care. You're hot, Morgan. Don't you know that?"

"You need glasses," she said.

"No, I don't. I mean, I do. But that's not the point."

"I'm not cutting anymore."

She was lying.

"Listen," I said. "That day on the football field, I saw you."

"I don't know what you're talking about."

"Yes, you do."

Morgan rubbed her eyes with the back of her hand. "Sometimes I just need to ... I can't explain. It's like a release, you know?"

I didn't know.

"Sure," I said. What else could I say?

"Don't judge me," she said.

"I'm not."

The wind kicked up, swirling leaves across the patio and flinging the rain sideways. I felt cold all of a sudden.

Morgan shivered. "Let's get out of here."

We left the pool and headed inside, dripping across the tile floor. It was pitch-dark in the house. I couldn't see where I was going. After a minute, my eyes adjusted, but nothing came into focus. I stumbled upstairs, and Morgan lagged behind.

I unfolded the hide-a-bed, tugged back the sheets, and climbed in. When I finally looked up, Morgan was standing there, naked. She climbed under the covers with me.

I didn't know what to do. How was I supposed to explain that I'd only had one girlfriend and we "dated" over the computer? It was pathetic, once you thought about it.

"Morgan," I whispered. "You can't stay here."

She scooted closer.

"Morgan," I said again.

"That's my name. Don't wear it out."

I couldn't help laughing. "You're something else. You know that?"

She shivered. "Right now, I'm freezing."

I wrapped the blanket tighter around us. Morgan nuzzled her face against mine. We were kissing again and her hands were sliding around.

"I can't do this," I told her.

She blinked at me. "You don't want to?"

"God. What do you think? Of course, I do. But it's just…"

"Just what?"

I could've told her the truth. *I've never done this before.* What difference would it make?

Morgan cried silently, her entire body shaking. "Be honest. You think I'm ugly."

"Stop it. Listen to me. You're not ugly, okay? Far from it."

"I can take a hint," she said, turning away from me.

I yanked back the covers. Morgan didn't move. Her scars were faint crosses rippling along her thighs. I moved my hands over them, tracing the raised surface of her skin.

"Believe me," I said.

Morgan pressed closer. It felt as if we were sinking underwater, drifting in slow-motion. I wanted to know if she cried when her stepmom punished her for writing with her left hand. I wondered what songs pumped through her headphones on the day we met, and did it hurt, the first time she dragged that piece of metal across her thigh, or did she learn to stop hurting, stop feeling anything at all. I knew that sex was supposed to be a big deal, but afterwards, we just lay there, barely touching.

That was the saddest part.

22 Close Your Eyes

It was too dark to see. No telling the time. Morgan snored with her head buried under the blanket. I wondered how she could breathe.

The door banged open, and Skully barged into the room. Her boots clicked across the floor. "You should see the backyard. A tree fell in the pool. Get up. I want to show you."

I shoved my face deeper into the pillow. Skully could be so evil sometimes.

She tickled my ear. "Did I disturb your peaceful slumber?"

"No," I mumbled.

"You can go back to sleep now."

"I'm not sleeping."

"So get up," she said.

"Give me a minute."

"Are you butt naked under there or what?" She tugged the blanket. It slipped out of my fingers. I scrambled for it, but she pulled it off the bed with a flourish. Her smile faded when she saw Morgan curled next to me, in nothing but her birthday suit.

"Oops," Skully said.

Morgan covered her eyes, as if that could make the room magically disappear. "Skully," she said. "Could you exit, stage left?"

"Sure thing."

"Like, right now?"

"You got it." She tripped over the blanket on the way out.

I groaned. "That did not just happen."

"Unfortunately, it did," Morgan said. "I saw everything... with my eyes closed."

"You realize that she's going to blab about this to everybody," I said, jerking the covers back on the bed. I draped it over us like a tent. We huddled under it like little kids in a fort.

"Are you embarrassed?" Morgan whispered.

I couldn't stop looking at her. "About what?"

"Do I have to spell it out?"

I leaned in for a kiss, but she moved away.

"You can do magic, right? Well, make my scars disappear," she said.

I shook my head. "Don't start this again."

"You're totally going to ignore me now, aren't you? I'll see you at school, and you'll pretend I don't exist."

"Do you really believe that?"

"I don't know."

"It sucks that you think so little of me. I mean, do you really think that I would just ditch you?"

"Wouldn't be the first time."

"I'm not like Brent or those other guys, okay?" I said. It sounded like a cheesy pickup line. "Just hear me out. I want you to know that last night was amazing."

"Then why aren't you smiling?" she asked.

"Look. There's a lot going on that you don't know about."

"Like what?"

"I can't tell you."

She frowned. "You're seeing somebody else."

"I'm not a player, if that's what you mean."

"Then what's so important that you can't talk about it?"

I kept my mouth shut.

She curled onto her side, away from me. "Brent was right."

"What's that supposed to mean?"

"He said you were fake."

Crap.

"What exactly did he say?"

"That you've been lying about a lot of things. He thinks you're just using people."

"And you believe him?"

Morgan did that cute thing, blowing her bangs off her forehead. "Maybe," she said.

I opened my mouth, but she was on a roll.

"Why were you living in that shitty apartment with your mom? Are you in trouble? Did you do something bad? Just tell me what's going on."

"I want to. You have no idea."

"Why can't you just tell me?"

"Because it could hurt you," I blurted out.

Morgan started to sob. "So it's true ... what Brent and all those people are saying." She cried harder. Her shoulders heaved. I put my arm around her but she pushed me away.

"Listen. I'm sorry you had to find out like this. I wanted to tell you, but it was never the right time. It wasn't even my idea."

She wiped her face. "What are you talking about?"

I'd blown it.

"You have no idea what I'm saying, do you?" I asked slowly.

"What did you think I meant? All that stuff people said about you being a player?"

"A player?" I shook my head. "I've never even had sex until last night."

"Right. I'm supposed to believe that? How can I believe anything you say?"

"It's true," I said. "I've never even had a real girlfriend."

"Is there something else I should know? Those rumors about you ... " She trailed off.

"Morgan, listen to me."

She was listening. And she already knew.

No use hiding anymore. I was sick of it. Sick of hiding, sneaking around, observing from a distance. Sick of keeping my mouth shut. For once, I opened it. This is what came out:

"I'm telling you the truth now, Morgan," I heard myself say. "I'm a narc. Do you understand what this means?"

She bit her lower lip. "Please tell me that this is a joke."

"I've been working undercover for the Miami Dade narcotics unit . . ."

"No," she said. "This is not happening."

" . . . and I'm supposed to find who's supplying to Palm Hammock."

Morgan stared at me, as if she could see through my skin, my bones, every molecule in my body.

"So tell me, Aaron—or whatever your name is—what's it like, working for the police?"

"It's not what you think," I said. "It was forced into it, you know? But now . . . I'm not sure what I'm doing."

"Well, maybe you can explain it to me."

"Listen. I really care about you. And Skully. Now that I've gotten to know you guys, I don't want to go through with this."

"But that's not going to stop you, is it?" she asked.

"I didn't want things to blow up like this. I didn't even send that invitation online. I don't know who e-mailed it to me. I told the lead officer that the alpha dog would be there."

"The what?"

"The guy who calls the shots. In this case, Finch. He's the one they want."

"Finch? What did he ever do to you? He's the sweetest guy on the planet."

"Right. The guy's got a dope farm in his garden shed."

"How do you know?"

"He and his dad were showing it off. But I can't figure him out. I think he's been trying to turn people against me. Remember that picture from Skully's party that got sent to the entire school?"

Morgan didn't say anything.

"The picture, remember?" I said. "The one where it looks like we're messing around."

"Of course. I know who took it."

I sat up straight. "Who?"

"Skully stole your phone. She confessed to me. I'm over it."

"Why the hell did she take that picture?"

"She was crushing on you. God. You're so stupid."

"Isn't she gay or whatever? How was I supposed to know?"

"I thought you were different from the other guys. I must've been insane."

"Morgan," I said, reaching for her. "You have to talk to me. This is really important, okay? What's the deal with the Everglades party?"

"I don't know who sent that message. I could totally

see Finch hacking into your account because he's real good at computers and stuff."

"He doesn't even go to our school. Why is he suspicious of me?"

"Because he figured it out."

"How?" I asked.

"You brought too much attention to yourself."

In my entire life, nobody had ever told me this.

"Like at Skully's party," she said. "You weren't into our scene, he never saw you at the house before. Then you start asking him for drugs. And you're, like, trying to buy a lot. Of course he's going to be suspicious."

My head was spinning. As the pieces of our conversation echoed in triple speed, my brain latched onto something worse:

"Do you think that Finch created this Everglades thing... to set me up?"

She pulled the sheet closer, although the room was warm, all of a sudden. Too warm. "If he knows what you're doing, then yes. He'll try to get rid of you."

"What do you think he'll do? How bad is it?" I asked.

"I don't know. But Finch never would've treated me like *this*."

"Right. What makes you think he's such a good guy?"

She glared. "We used to go out."

"Unbelievable," I said. Finch, with the snarly hair and gross mustache. "God. Who else have you slept with?"

Morgan slipped out of the bed. She shrugged into her prairie dress, leaving the buttons undone, and bolted down the spiral staircase. I raced after her, half-tripping because I couldn't see shit. I pounded down the steps, around and around, calling her name.

There was nothing I could say, except, "I'm sorry," but she wouldn't listen.

When I reached the last step, I looked out through the sliding glass door at the pool, and even without my glasses, I could see that a tree had fallen into it: either torched by lightning or toppled by the wind. A thicket of leaves clogged the deep end. I should've gone out there and pushed the tree back into place, but I knew it wouldn't budge.

I just wasn't strong enough.

———

Status: UNSENT
To: LadyM
From: Metroid
Subject: (No Subject)

Dear Morgan,
I'm sorry.
I tried calling you a million times, but you won't pick up. Just let me explain. If you ever talk to me again, it will all make sense. I swear. Please don't shut me out. The Internet is dead. I even walked to the Starbucks on Old Cutler (in a

lame attempt to borrow their Wi-Fi, but when I didn't buy anything, they kicked me out).

Now I'm at Skully's house. She keeps asking me about you. I think she knows I fucked up, but I guess you didn't tell her that the party's a setup. And don't worry. I won't tell her anything about last night. I'm good at keeping my mouth shut. You could say I'm an expert at it. Besides. I'm not one of those guys who runs around bragging about their "conquests" or whatever. As I've already told you, my lack of experience is a joke. Who am I kidding? My whole life is a joke.

If you were here, you would look into my eyes and know I'm telling the truth. The cops straight up played me. I swear to God. Do you really think I wanted to go through with this? It's supposed to be my senior year. I didn't need this shit dumped on me. I only did it because they threatened my little sister. I can't let anything happen to her. My mom is basically AWOL, and I'm the only one around.

I had to make a choice.

Please don't think I'm laying excuses on you. I mean, it doesn't justify what I did. It fucking sucks, but that's the way it is. You deserve soooo much better. I want you back in my life. I need to believe that's possible.

So I'm sitting on the bed at Skully's. Holding back tears. Listening to my iPod. Every song reminds me of you. I miss the forest-smell of your hair. I miss holding you in my arms. I remember that night on the roof. Your Wintergreen kiss. The first party, when you put a rubber band on my wrist. The field at school. You: sitting on the bleachers like an Egyptian queen. God, I wish I could go back in time.

I miss your everything.

—A.

PART THREE

23 All Hallows

The cars arrived at Skully's an hour before sundown. I heard their doors slam before I looked through the kitchen window. About a half-dozen seniors from Palm Hammock were flicking cigarettes into the ferns. All of them wore costumes, from plastic masks to full-blown gorilla suits.

"Who the hell are those fools?" I asked Skully.

She dipped in front of me and lowered the blinds. The room grew darker. "Morgan's customers," she said.

"So tell them she's not here. Shit. Do you realize that if you get caught, you're in huge trouble? What if someone rats you out, that there are drug deals going on here? The cops would drag your ass to jail. Your parents could lose their house."

"Chill. Nothing's going to happen. They're looking for a party. Just ignore them and they'll take off."

I was still thinking about Morgan, wondering exactly what she said, and what was going to happen to us. By now, she had probably told everybody. It doesn't take long for stuff to get around, especially if you've got a cell phone or an Internet connection. Then again, if she had blown my cover, why were all these people showing up at the house, getting ready to head out for the Glades party?

I thought about the big bust the entire freaking narcotics unit was planning for the Everglades party. What if Morgan told Finch not to show? My sister . . . God. What if he came after her? I couldn't let that happen.

There was no way I could talk everyone out of this Everglades party. But maybe, just maybe I could steer the cops away from the girls. It was Finch they wanted, anyway. And if we didn't catch the shot caller, we were all in danger. I racked my brain trying to find an answer.

It was like those cartoons where there's an angel sitting on your right shoulder and a devil on your left. Stay or go? Bail out or stick around? I couldn't decide what to do. I looked at Skully and her little brother. They had no clue what was in store for them. I'd made a promise to keep them safe and though I was nobody's definition of a hero, I was man enough to admit one thing:

I couldn't let my friends get hurt.

The sky had turned molten. No more rain. I thought

of a rhyme Dad used to say: *Red sky at night, sailors delight. Red sky in the morning, sailors take warning.*

More people had parked on the neighbor's freshly mowed lawn. They wore Dracula capes and bandit masks. Cowboy hats. Fairy wings. One guy showed up in a bed sheet, stirring the crowd to chant, "Toga, toga!"

They read about the party in text message. An e-mail. A bulletin online. It seemed like the entire school was parked on Skully's lawn. I didn't recognize half the faces, but they kept looking at me. I waved. A few waved back. Most just stared.

"I have to put on my costume," Skully said.

Then a pickup truck rolled into the driveway, the gravel snap, crackle, popping, just like Morgan said at my first party, which felt like centuries ago. The truck had blimp-sized tires fit to wade through mud, and it was dragging a boat behind it. Even with my outdated-prescription glasses, I recognized it right off the bat. The airboat belonged to Finch, the guy in the driver's seat.

He beeped the horn. "How's it going?"

I nodded back at him.

"You know Brent, right?" he said, jerking his thumb at another truck. The window rolled down and Brent's face appeared, his expression unreadable.

"Yeah. I know him," I said.

"You guys are supposed to be wearing costumes," Skully said, reappearing. She was decked out in combat boots, a skin-tight dress, and a pair of strap-on angel wings.

"So where's your disguise?" Finch asked.

Skully flipped him off. "Go to hell."

"Sure thing," he said, turning the truck around. For a second, I thought he'd shoved a hat on the back of his head. No. A papier-mâché devil's mask: the kind you buy off a rack at Party City. Brent had the same thing.

"What cheap-ass costumes," Sebastian called out, coming up behind us.

"Better than those pajamas you're wearing," Finch said.

"I'm a ninja." Sebastian pulled a hood over his head. "See?"

"Looks more like the Grim Reaper." Finch tossed a cigarette out the window. "And who are you supposed to be?" he asked me. "Clark Kent?"

"My costume is invisible."

"Okay, boys," Skully said. "Enough yakking. We've got to jet before it gets dark. What happened to Morgan?"

"She's at her place, getting ready," Brent said. "You know how that goes."

He gave me this weird look, like he was eavesdropping on my mind. Finch gunned the truck, spraying gravel all over the lawn. Soon we were following him in the Skullymobile. Sebastian rode shotgun. I huddled in the backseat, checking e-mail on my cell every two seconds.

SUBJECT: AARON

Somebody had forwarded a message to me. At first, I thought it was one of those chain letters, the type that tell you to send this to ten people and you'll have good luck for the rest of the day. Or whatever. As I scrolled down, I realized it was one of those cut and paste deals, where everyone keeps adding comments to the list. And it was about me.

"I had Aaron in my math class. I always thought he was a little weird," wrote a girl named emily1995. I didn't know anyone named Emily. How could she call me "weird" when we never talked?

I kept reading.

"Honestly, I have mixed feelings about him," said another girl (if it was, in fact, a girl) named Special K.

How could they judge me? Just look at their idiotic screen names. Nobody goes around calling themselves Special K.

I scrolled down more. The entire e-mail sounded like a chatroom. *"There's no way he's a narc. He hangs with chicks all the time. That's so gay,"* wrote a guy who called himself Hercules.

My hands were shaking. I couldn't hit the "off" button. By accident, I clicked on one of my bookmarked links. On the Facebook page, I saw a dozen crappy cell phone pictures posted on "my" wall. Me: driving to school. Eating a corndog in the lunchroom. Running laps in gym class. Smoking a clove with Skully. Carrying Morgan up the stairs, piggyback-style.

"He's kind of hot, actually," wrote someone I actually knew. Danica Stone. I clicked over to her Facebook profile and scrolled down.

"Couple of random things... might go 2 that Glades party, but who knows what ur mom will say."

She'd probably say, "Learn to spell."

I clicked through her photos. My only defender was a girl who listed Artie Abrams from *Glee* as her hero and who couldn't tell the difference between the letter O and the number zero.

In the front seat, Skully kept talking about my levitation trick. How cool it was when I pulled "badass magic" on Brent. How she's totally going to learn street magic like that middle-aged Goth guy on TV.

"Double A, will you teach me some street magic?" Skully asked.

"Not while you're driving."

Sebastian handed me a quarter. "Can you show me how to pull this out of somebody's ear?"

I bounced the coin across my knuckles. "Later."

"So how did you learn magic?" he asked. "By watching videos on YouTube or something?"

"No, I read those square things called books."

Skully turned on the radio. "What's with you, Double A? Are you pissed off because of all the drama with Morgan? She'll be there later."

I wasn't sure if I wanted Morgan to show up at the party or not. I glanced down at my phone. Another e-mail popped up. When I clicked on it, I almost choked.

"Faker," it said. *"I hope you die."*

I hit delete.

"Double A?" Skully said. "Hello?"

"I just need to close my eyes, okay?" I tugged the hood of my sweatshirt around my head like a monk.

"Okey doke," she muttered.

I'd hurt her feelings. Soon I was going to hurt everybody, even the people who never talked to me, the ones who drifted through the halls and stared without saying hello. They'd look at me and whisper. They didn't have the guts to speak to my face, to be real for once, to come clean.

I had to go through with this. There was no turning back. No choice left to make. I couldn't just let the girls walk into a trap, but I wasn't sure I could tell Skully and Sebastian the truth either. Not if it meant even the slightest chance of Finch discovering me. I was still hoping for a chance to catch him without getting the girls sucked into the mess. I'd have to stay close and get them out before it was too late.

Nobody was going to save them.

It was all up to me.

24 No Fences

Skully drove with the windows rolled down. We headed west on 8th Street, otherwise known as the Tamiami Trail, a name I recognized from the message online. A sign read *U-Pick Tomatoes* on a plot of land filled with nothing but dirt. Plastic chairs sat beside a canal where nobody fished.

"Feels like the end of the world," I said.

My brain was going crazy. I couldn't stop thinking about Morgan and what we did last night. It felt like a scene from TV instead of something that actually happened. I wanted to hold her again. Cover her with my hands, the only part of me that seemed real. But even my hands were liars.

Sebastian kept bugging me to show him a coin trick. "Teach it to me. Please? Or else, give me back my quarter."

He stuck his head through the window. "Check it. That tree looks like a Chia Pet. It's like a stuffed animal. Except that leaves grow out of it. Is it just me, or do you smell fire?"

"It's just you," his sister said.

I tried to tune them out, but Skully cranked up the radio. She and Sebastian sang along, snapping their fingers.

"Hey, Double A," Skully said. "Can you snap your fingers in a Z?"

I smiled, but she could tell something was off.

"You're megaquiet today," she said. "Not yourself at all."

"How would you know?" I mumbled. "We've only been hanging out for a couple months."

"That's all it takes."

If only that were true.

"I'm so glad I got to know you this year," she said.

That's when I couldn't take it anymore. Morgan already knew, so what difference would it make? My head was going to explode. The words got stuck in my throat. Then I told them what I'd wanted to say the whole time:

The truth.

"Listen," I said. "This is going to sound weird, but we need to watch our backs tonight."

"What?" She turned down the radio.

"The cops are out for Finch. They've been trying to find the guy who's supplying to the school. Get it? This party is an undercover bust."

Skully scraped out a laugh. "Right. A police sting in the Everglades. How do you know all this?"

"Because I've been helping them."

She stopped laughing. Her face toggled between emotions: confusion, fear, and then a flicker of doubt. "Are you punking me? That's not funny. You better not be making this up."

"I swear. I've never been more real in my life." I blinked and wiped my eyes. This was worse than I imagined.

The car swerved as Skully pulled off the road. She didn't say a word. There was only the sound of her keys, clacking back and forth.

"I thought it was a joke," she finally said. "All those people talking shit about you. I mean, yeah, I know what that's like. Now you're saying it's true?"

"Please hear me out. I only did this because I got dragged into it. They were going to arrest my little sister. And now the cops are saying if this plan falls through, Finch and his boys will be looking for revenge. They'll come after Haylie next. You don't understand. I would do anything to keep her safe. Anything…"

Skully stared. "I believe you," she said softly.

"You do?"

She glanced at her brother. "Yeah. I do."

"What's going to happen now?" Sebastian asked. He looked so scared, I couldn't help reaching across the seat and snatching his hand.

"They're going to throw us in jail. That's what," Skully

said. "You're telling me it's only about Finch, but the cops don't care. They'll arrest everybody."

"Then we should turn around. Now," Sebastian said.

"So you're just going to bail?" I asked. "Sorry. I can't do that."

"You're either really brave or really crazy," he said.

Brave? He didn't know how far that was from the truth.

"I'm working on a plan to keep you out of it. Safe," I told them. The same thing I told Morgan in the letter I never sent.

"What should we do?" Skully asked.

"First of all, keep your mouth shut. You can't let anyone find out. I mean anyone. Morgan already knows. The less people know, the better."

"Deal," she said.

"And when the cops show up?" Sebastian didn't seem convinced. "What are we supposed to do?"

"Leave it to me," I told them.

———————

In the backseat, I watched the windows. As we sped closer to the Glades, we passed a shopping cart glinting in tall grass. Bird nests on telephone poles. A teddy bear strapped to a tree where somebody had crashed and died.

"Have you driven down here before?" I asked.

Skully nodded. "Lots of times."

I put away the Sandman graphic novel that I found on the floor. I'd scanned the same page five times.

At last, we bumped along a dirt road. The Hummer barged through the sawgrass, parting it like the tide. The other cars drifted ahead: brake lights flashing along the path. A message in Morse Code: *we're in trouble.*

Skully cut the engine.

"Now what?" I asked.

She took out a rhinestone-studded mirror and smeared lipstick around her smile. "We walk."

I followed her through the sawgrass. The knife-sharp edges whipped against my pants. I locked onto Skully's angel wings, which bobbed like a living thing strapped to her back. Every noise made me shudder, all the buzzing in the pines.

"What's that sound? It's freaking me out," I said.

"Just frogs and cicadas," said Sebastian, loping ahead with his plastic ninja sword.

"What about gators?" I asked, darting a glance into the canal.

"You're looking at one. Those things are everywhere," he said.

I squinted. A log came into focus. Not a log. A tail.

"Shit," I said.

The gator sat so quiet and still, I wouldn't have noticed until Sebastian pointed it out.

"Is it dead?" I asked.

Sebastian laughed. "Nope. He's chillaxin."

I stopped for a second and studied the gator's eyes,

which rose like a periscope in the mud-colored water. They closed ever so slowly, the lids thin as tissue paper.

"We used to see way more gators. But with last summer's drought and everything, they're basically drying up."

"Yuck. They scare me," Skully said. "I hope they become extinct."

"He's just doing his job," I said softly, unable to look away.

"He or she," Skully added.

"As long as you can run thirty miles per hour, you're cool," Sebastian said.

Skully picked up the pace. "Can we change the subject? Keep walking."

"He probably thinks you're a big bird."

"La. La. La," she sang. "I'm not listening."

We caught up with the others, who had gathered in a circle close to the water's edge. I kept waiting for someone to call me out. After reading all my hate mail online, I didn't know what to expect.

I spotted Finch's devil mask. He had an old-fashioned holster slung across his chest. I wondered if the gun was loaded.

Brent was there, too, pretending to be a pirate, saying things like "Thar she blows" or just snarling "Argh" every five seconds. Everybody laughed, as if this were actually funny. Of course, everything is a riot when you're stoned. I walked closer to Brent.

"Are the girls here?" I asked him.

Brent flipped his eye patch from one side to the other. "You mean Skully? Oh, she doesn't count as a girl." He laughed.

Finch cut between us. "Looking for Morgan? Haven't seen her yet."

Just the sound of him drawling her name was enough to make me want to puke. How could she have ever hooked up with this tool? He offered me a beer, but I waved it away.

"Suit yourself," he said, taking a swig.

Sebastian said, "Let me have a taste."

Finch passed him the can.

I dug my fingers into my palms. I was going to destroy this guy, no matter how the night panned out.

Finch lead us to the airboat. He and Brent unloaded it off the trailer into the water. Once the airboat had splashed into the canal, we were good to go.

Only a few people could ride at one time. I let the others giggle and stumble aboard while I hung back with Skully and her brother. Where was Morgan? Was she ever going to show up?

A girl with a Mardi Gras mask approached me. "Hey," she said, as if we were long lost buddies.

"Hey, yourself," I said.

She squatted down on the grass. "So you're Aaron, right?"

I cringed. "Who wants to know?"

"Danica."

"Danica Stone?"

"The one and only."

With her hair scraped back and her face hidden behind the mask, I didn't recognize the chick. She had a nice body, packed into skinny jeans, and it was pretty obvious she wasn't wearing a bra. No wonder the girls hated her.

Danica tugged off her mask. Up close, she was even hotter. Her skin was smooth and tan, and when she turned her face, specks of glitter caught the light across her cheekbones.

"Where's your costume?" she asked.

"It's a secret costume."

"Can I see it?"

"Maybe later," I said, as Skully pulled me away.

"Why are you talking to that skank?" she whispered.

"She seems nice."

"That's because you're a boy."

The airboat's fan chugged to life, making a noise like a million hornets. All the girls nearby covered their ears and shrieked in fake fear.

"You ready for this?" Skully asked.

We looked at each other. The secret hung between us.

"Ready as I'll ever be."

"Good," she said. "Because we're next."

25 Island

The airboat wobbled as we climbed aboard. By this time, the sun had set. I could hardly see the trees, much less whatever was lurking in the water.

"Hang on guys. This is only the second time I've driven this thing," Finch said, waving a flashlight as if we were at the planetarium.

"Liar," Skully said.

He reached into a metal basket under the seat and pulled out a bag of cotton balls. "I never lie," he said, tossing it at me. "Isn't that true?"

I looked at the puddles of mud on the floor, then the cotton balls. "Are we making arts and crafts?"

"Stuff them in your ears. Unless you want to go deaf."

The sun had dipped behind the pines, but there was

enough light to see another gator stretched on the grass like a lawn ornament.

"Oh, my god," Skully said. "It's smiling at me."

Finch grinned. "Red is their favorite color."

Skully patted her Kool-Aid auburn hair and groaned.

I leaned back as the boat flew across the canal. We glided into the open water, swerving around clumps of tall grass and mile after mile of tangled lilies. I clung to the bench and kept watch for alligator eyes.

"Oh shit. Forgot to fill the gas tank," Finch joked as the motor rumbled to a halt and we could hear again.

"Funny." I pinched out the cotton balls and listened to the frogs barking in the weeds. No traffic noises, no planes. Just a spooky kind of quiet after the roar of the boat.

One at a time, we scrambled out of the boat onto a muddy beach covered in footprints from the previous boatloads of kids. Hard to tell where the swamp ended and dry land began. Finch clamped a flashlight between his teeth and beckoned us into the woods.

Skully grabbed my hand. Her grip tightened as a flock of storks took to the sky, folding their wings like origami. "God, that scared the crap out of me."

My cell phone rumbled in my pocket.

"What the hell was that?" she asked.

"Somebody sent a text," I said, slipping it out halfway, trying to read the message. It was from the lead officer.

Are you ready?

"You've got service out here? Damn," she said.

"It comes and goes."

"Use it while you've got the chance. It's only going to get worse."

True.

I wiped the sweat off my forehead.

"Who was that, anyway?" she asked.

"A friend," I said, hoping she caught my drift. "He wants to join us, but I'm not exactly sure where we're at."

"Me neither," she said. "Just tell him we're near the park entrance."

"Yeah, but ... how is he going to get here?"

I crammed the phone back in my pocket. I still couldn't decide what to do. I dug out the quarter I'd been carrying ever since Sebastian passed it to me in the car. I tossed the coin and flipped it over. Tails.

"You never taught me that magic trick," Skully said.

"I told you. There's no magic to it. You just stick a coin in someone's ear and pretend to pull it out."

"That's it?"

"Well, yeah. You just act like it was there all along."

"And people fall for that," she said. "Why?"

"They'll believe anything, if they want it to be true."

"Next you'll tell me that the Tooth Fairy isn't real," she said, pouting.

I waited until she walked ahead, then I took out my cell and sent the magic words:

All the players are here.

I didn't even need to relay the exact address. If 911 could track a location from a cell phone signal, so could the narcotics team. The lead officer would pass it to a select group of police. He said it could take them an hour to get briefed, assemble a team, and load the vehicles. They were waiting to crank up the "foot soldiers," also known as "troops."

Let the lead officer figure out the rest.

Skully turned around. "Double A? You coming?"

"Yeah," I called back.

We made our way into a clearing. Somebody had built a bonfire, which must've been illegal on all sorts of levels. The others had crowded around it: Sebastian, guzzling another can of beer, and Brent, the designated DJ, messing with a boom box. It wasn't so much a "party" as a "gathering."

Finch had his arm around some girl. She was so small, he practically had to bend in half just to whisper in her ear. She looked like a junior high kid, clutching a beer, trying to look sexy in a cheerleading skirt. I did a double take and realized who it was.

Haylie.

What the hell was she doing with Finch? I was losing my cool.

"Haylie! Get over here," I yelled, like I was her dad or something.

"What are you doing here?" She glared at me. "Whatever. Go away, Aaron. Leave me alone. Don't act like you're so perfect."

God. Now my little sister hated me, too. She was my reason for all of this. And she didn't even know it.

Finch dangled a blunt in front of my face and grinned mockingly. I took it and inhaled. Held the smoke as long as possible. Coughed my brains out.

Finch clapped me on the back. "How's that blunt treating you?"

"I swear to god. If you so much as touch my sister—"

"You guys are gross." Haylie wrinkled her nose. "I need to pee," she said, heading for the bushes.

I tried to follow her, but soon as I was lost in a maze of straggly-looking pine trees. I stopped. That's when I noticed Morgan, sitting above me on a branch. What was she doing here? She knew what was up.

Morgan wore a crown on her head and a long nightgown that flowed in the breeze. When she noticed me, a rush of guilt swept through my chest. I wanted to make things right, but it wasn't going to happen.

I was thinking. That is, thinking about calling her name. If we were going to talk, it had to happen naturally. No sooner had the thought crossed my mind, when I realized that I hadn't planned on talking at all. I was prepared to follow my usual course of action: ignoring her because it hurt too much to talk. But I couldn't run away this time. Maybe I could give her a quick explanation before bolting. Even that sounded lame.

Morgan pushed back her hair, held in place by a sparkly

crown, the kind a Disney princess would wear. It caught the light and sprayed diamonds across her forehead.

"I didn't think you'd show," I said, craning my neck to look at her. A stupid thing to say.

Morgan scowled. "Nice costume."

"I'm not wearing one."

"Not true."

"Look. We've got to talk," I said.

"Okay." She still didn't move.

"Um. This is kind of awkward."

"I can't hear you." She extended her hand, as if she could pull me into the tree.

Back near the bonfire, a few people shouted at us. I ignored them and unlaced my sneakers. It was easier, climbing barefoot. I grabbed the lowest branch and hauled myself up, slipping a little as I got closer. The branches weren't smooth. They were furry with moss. Once I found my balance, I swung myself over a limb and prayed I didn't break my neck.

Skully called out from the edge of the party crowd, "Morgan and Aaron sitting in a tree..."

"You're a coward," Morgan said.

"Don't say that."

"Isn't it true?"

"What the fuck, Morgan? You have no idea what I've been through."

"You?" she said. "Why don't you go back to wherever you came from and stop fucking with my life?"

"I didn't want this job. I got roped into it. Now I wish I never came here. But I'm also glad I did it. I got to see things in a different light, you know? Start over."

"Yeah. By faking it."

"Everybody is fake," I said. "That's what school is all about. If you don't fake your way through it, you won't survive."

"That's bullshit and you know it," she said. "You ratted us out."

"Then why did you come?"

"For them." She peered back at the others. "They wouldn't listen. They just think, 'Oh, crazy Morgan. She had a fight with some boy.' All those rumors, but they wouldn't believe it was true when I told them."

"Told them what?"

"That you're a narc."

I glanced at the fire, wishing I could be there, with the others, laughing. Not knowing what was coming. I watched Finch lift a branch from the flames and raise it high, like a torch. Through my tunnel vision I could see that the old-fashioned gun was still strapped to his belt.

"He's not your friend, you know. He's waiting to take you down," Morgan said.

I refocused on her and pulled out my cell. "See this? It was given to me by the cops. Once I figured out that Finch was calling the shots, I could have bailed. But I didn't."

"Am I supposed to believe that? How can I believe anything you say?"

"I could call them right now."

"You don't even know where you are," she said.

And she was right. "Fuck you. I'm so over this."

I jumped down, landing on all fours. Pain zinged through my knees, but I barely noticed it. There must have been something else cut into that blunt I smoked earlier. I stared at the tree, and it seemed to quiver.

"Shit."

I tried to focus on the maze of branches. Anything to steady myself. But it wasn't just my old glasses messing up my vision. Now the leaves were multiplying. I looked at Morgan, perched there, and it's as if I knew what was cooking in her mind. I looked at the bonfire, the people in costumes huddled around it, and I knew their thoughts, too. I took out my cell again and pictured the radio waves lacing the air. The phone was poison. I chucked it, as far as possible, into the bushes. I grunted loudly as it crashed, and everyone stared.

"Have a good look," I shouted. "Go on, you poseurs. All you fake-ass people. I know what you're thinking. Why don't you say it to my face?"

"Not here," Finch said, stepping out from the group of people. "You wanna talk, little piggy? Let's roll." He stood and brushed the ashes off his jeans.

"Fine," I told him. I had to do this, even if he beat the shit out of me. It was my chance to lead Finch away from the girls. Where the hell were the cops already?

Morgan screamed, "Don't go," but everything had dimmed to a blurry distance. I was floating high above it.

Her voice faded away. The fire shrank to a pinpoint. Finch marched ahead, snapping branches into my face. I kept walking, only looking at his back in front of me. When we finally reached a clearing, he stood near the water, as if considering a dip.

"I'm gonna speak real slow, cause I know that pigs have a hard time understanding plain English," he said. "You got two choices. Run. Or swim."

"Thought we were going to talk."

"Why should I listen to a smartass narc who butts into other people's business? I'm making some mad cash flow here, but I ain't hurting nobody. Just give the rich bitches what they want. A little Mary J. A little Kryppie. If they don't buy from me, they'll score it somewhere else. At least I didn't jack their trust, the way you did. Pretend to be tight with the homies." He dragged out the word. "Did you get any play from it, man? Did Morgan put out? Or Skully? Or did you bang them both?"

I swung at his face with my now tingling arm, but Finch dodged it easily. My knees wobbled. The trees bent and spun. Then Finch slammed a roundhouse punch into my chest. I staggered back, wheezing. He knocked the wind out of me again. I sank to the ground. When I finally summoned the strength to lift my head, I saw Brent coming toward me with a stick.

"Brent," I called out.

He pivoted, like he was going to nail a golf ball, and the stick smashed into my shoulder, ripping through my shirt and skin with the rough bark. I groaned as Brent pummeled me over and over until I blacked out for a moment. I spat a mouthful of blood and dirt and squinted at the two boys towering over me. Finch was actually filming this with a mini DV camera. No doubt he would post the footage over the Internet and brag about beating the shit out of the narc.

Finch passed the camera to Brent. They laughed and mumbled, stepped back and surveyed the damage. They were drunk, but I was no match for the two of them, especially after smoking that A-bomb and whatever Finch cut into it.

"Hey, Captain Save-A-Ho," Brent said, aiming the camera in my face. "Smile."

My ribs ached. Every muscle in my body thudded with dull pain. Tiny white fireworks exploded in front of my eyes.

"That's enough," Brent said. "Just leave him. It's over."

Finch reached for his gun. "It ain't over yet."

"Come on," Brent said.

Finch waved the gun at him. "Get out of the way."

Brent opened his mouth, but changed his mind. "Hurry up and waste that god damned snitch."

"I got a better idea." Finch shoved the gun at Brent. "You do it."

Now Brent was shaking so hard, he couldn't keep the

gun steady. Finch wrestled the camera away and pointed it at me.

I looked up at Brent, trying to read his zombie expression, and thought about the time we played video games together, that night at the gallery. That thing he said about his dad hitting him. All the rage inside him. Then me and Finch, shooting targets in the backyard. Bet this didn't seem any different to them.

"Brent," I said, hoping he'd snap out of it. He looked at the gun, then at me. Behind him, the bushes snapped and rustled, and there was Haylie, barging her way toward us. She had no clue what was going on. She just stood there in her stupid cheerleader costume. I saw her face change as she slowly figured out that I was in trouble. That we were all in trouble.

Brent turned near Haylie, the gun still in his grip.

Finch snatched it away from him and took aim at me.

"Stop it, stop it," Haylie screamed, running to me.

I lunged to my feet and tried to stop Haylie.

He fired.

The blast kicked up sand near my head. I flinched at the burst of light and noise.

Another blast. The gun went off and Haylie staggered back. She sank down, crumpled in the dirt, her mouth open in a silent shriek.

If I ever hoped to run away, there was no chance in hell now. White hot pain bloomed throughout my entire body. Somebody was screaming. It took a second before I realized it was me.

Finch shot again. His aim was off, which was surprising because he stood at point-blank range. He gazed into the distance, then he bolted.

I mustered enough energy to crane my head, and then it was clear why Finch ran.

The trees were burning.

26 Swamp Rats

I was bleeding in the sand, watching the flames twist and curl against the horizon. Even from a distance, the heat was intense. My arm was scraped, my glasses gone. I managed to drag myself closer to the shoreline, but what good would it do? There was no place to go.

Birds of all shapes and sizes scattered across the sky. I choked and gagged on the minty smoke. All the wet burning plants leaked poison into the air. My eyes watered as I tried to make out shapes in the pines.

This was my fault. I'd barged my way into other people's lives, just like Finch said. They had confided in me, trusted me with their secrets, and I'd turned my back on them. I just never imagined it would go this far. I thought I was doing something good. I saw myself as a peaceful warrior, but now I couldn't tell what was right or wrong, real or fake.

I kept my eyes on the birds rocketing in every direction, and they were the most amazing things I'd ever seen. For once, I didn't have to think. I could just lie there. All of a sudden, I was so damned tired.

Where was my sister? That's the only thought that brought me back to reality. What if she got hurt? Or worse. God, this was all my fault. If anyone deserved to die, it was me.

Somebody grabbed my hand. I must've been already dead because I was looking at an angel, wings and all. Only it wasn't an angel. Skully. And she wasn't alone. Haylie was there, too, and behind her, Morgan.

Haylie's sleeve was stained dark just above her left bicep. A bullet must've grazed her skin. Shit. I snapped back to reality. Even with a shallow wound, it was dangerous, losing that much blood. We had to stop the bleeding. Fast.

"My brother is missing," Skully said. Her face was slick with tears.

"Listen. He's here somewhere. First we need to make a tourniquet," I told Haylie.

Haylie sat on the ground. "Everything is spinning."

"Just sit tight. Try not to move." I tugged my sweatshirt over my head. This was bad. Really bad. I folded the sleeves and clamped down on Haylie's arm until the bleeding slowed a bit.

"They taught us how to do this in Health class," she said. "We need a stick so we can tie the sweatshirt around it."

"That's right," I said. Her voice shrank away. All I heard was a metallic ringing in my ears.

Morgan appeared with a tree branch. She helped me tie the tourniquet. The girls were putting up a decent front, but I knew they were freaking out. To be honest, I was, too.

"The shoreline is the safest place right now," I said. "Do you think we can get over there?"

The girls plunged into the water, Skully helping Haylie hold her bandaged arm out of the dirty water. There was no telling what was lurking in it. Gators and snakes. Morgan sobbed quietly. Her dress swelled like a parachute as we treaded farther out. I bent down and kissed her, though I knew this wasn't exactly the right time.

We held each other as the fire raged in the swamp. Plumes of pale smoke rose as solid as columns.

"Somebody's coming," Skully said. She waded back toward the shore, then stopped as another figure appeared.

Sebastian limped toward us. His face was pale and sweating. Just looking at him, I knew he was sick. He clutched his stomach and groaned.

"Oh, my god. Did you drink alcohol?" Skully was near-hysterical, frozen in place.

"Hey, you're bleeding," he said to Haylie. His words were slurry and faint.

"You know you're not supposed to drink. Are you

insane? Your blood sugar just crashed and now your numbers are wrecked. Where's your flash-lancing thingie?"

"I forgot it," he said.

She whipped around to us. "Does anyone have candy on them? Anyone? Please tell me. Someone's got to have candy."

Nobody moved.

Sebastian wasn't alone. Brent stood behind him, his face twisted with fear.

I reached out and we pulled Sebastian into the water. Skully sobbed as she clung to her brother. I glanced at Brent, and he looked away.

"You're a piece of shit," he told me.

"Okay. Fine. What happened to everybody?"

"They took the airboat."

"Where's Finch?" I asked.

"Gone," Brent said.

"You mean, they ditched you?"

Brent stared at the murky surface. "No way am I going in there."

"We have to keep moving," Morgan told him.

He didn't budge. The girls tried to grab his hands, but he shook them off.

"Just go," he said.

Morgan looked at Brent, then at me.

"Come on," I said, taking her hand.

We left him behind on the shore and sank deeper into the muck, inching our way through the tangled lilies. Who knew how much longer we could keep paddling? It wasn't that deep, but I'd heard stories about kids drowning in the weeds, if the gators didn't snatch them first. Haylie would be the first to go, since she was the smallest and bleeding.

"What's going to happen to us?" Morgan asked.

I gave her a squeeze. "It's cool. Everything's cool," I whispered. Another lie, but at that moment, I almost believed it.

After sloshing around in circles for a while, I couldn't figure out if we had gone the same way before. Without a flashlight or a fire, the Everglades have a way of swallowing you up. When the girls wandered too far ahead, they disappeared, as if the blackness hadn't simply covered them, but zapped them to another dimension. Luckily they stopped until we could see them again.

"This is insane," said Morgan, clutching her purse under one arm and punching buttons on her cell. "There's no bars on my stupid phone. Nobody knows we're here."

"Not true. The cops are looking for us right now. Maybe they sent out a search unit." I was holding back tears, trying to keep it together. "It wasn't supposed to happen this way."

"When I saw you at school, I knew there was something weird about you," she said. "I just didn't know what it was. You didn't have a clique, so I thought, maybe you just hung out with whoever you wanted. And I was like, 'That's cool.

He's doing his own thing.' Now I look back and see how fake you were. You're not really friends with anyone."

Her words stung. Did I really come across like that?

Skully said, "I let you stay at my place. I thought you were in trouble."

Only Sebastian stuck up for me. "He's been through everything and he hasn't ratted us out, right?"

I didn't know what to say. Because technically I had.

"Right?" he asked again.

The sound of splashing water caught my attention. I turned and saw a shadow drifting towards us. An airboat. Did Finch come back? Or did the narcotics team bust their way through the swamp?

"It's the cops," Sebastian said.

I watched the boat zigzag until I saw a group of men crouched on the prow, shining their flashlights. They wore loose-fitting jeans and patchwork shirts. The oldest guy had knotted his silvery hair into a ponytail that flopped over his shoulder like a sash.

"What do we have here?" he said, peering down at the girls.

The man behind him, the one with gold hoops glinting in both ears, said, "Looks like a bunch of swamp rats."

"Are you going to arrest us?" Haylie asked.

The men laughed.

"What for?" the older guy asked. "Something you wanna confess?"

"The fire," I told them. "I think it's our fault."

The older guy laughed harder. "That what you think? Who started it in the first place?"

I chewed my lip. "You?"

"That's right. It's our land, not the park's. Always has been our land. This here is a controlled burn."

"Controlled burn?" I echoed. Talk about a contradiction.

"Cleans out the non-native plants, the invasive species."

Invasive.

"Burns all the hammock scrub that doesn't belong here, you know? So they don't suffocate the pines. When we saw your little campfire, we thought the burn had spread."

The man held out his meaty fingers. I reached for them, and he helped me scramble onto the boat. They had a dog on board, a slobbering mutt. The beast leaped at me, slamming its paws on my chest and nearly knocking me overboard.

"Don't worry. She don't bite ... hard," the older guy said.

We helped weak Sebastian up next, then together we pulled the girls onto the boat, one at a time.

"Do you have any candy on you?" Skully asked.

The older guy blinked. "That's a strange question. Actually, I've got a chocolate bar in the cooler. Will that do?"

"Yes," she said, smiling at her brother. "It will do just fine."

"Any more of you swamp rats?" asked the guy with the gold hoops.

I nodded. "Our friend is still on the island."

"Then you better hang tight," said the older guy. "We

heard noises, smelled smoke. Were you shooting guns out here or just fireworks?"

Nobody said anything.

We sped back where we started. It didn't take long to find Brent, standing waist-deep in the water, a few feet away from the shore. When he saw the airboat, he just stood there, as if he couldn't believe his eyes. Haylie seemed to have sobered up and looked really tired now. Whatever Finch had laced into the joint he gave me had worn off as well. The girls huddled under blankets, and Sebastian was clinging to the dog, his arms cradled around its neck. So I slid into the water and waded toward Brent.

"It's over," I told him.

Brent looked at me and started to sob.

I held out my hand, but he didn't take it. Just moved past me, as if I didn't exist.

I was gone now. Disappeared. Erased.

The smoke rose higher, seeping into my clothes, my hair, my throat.

It would never wash out.

27 Eden

The men were from a tribe of Miccosukee who made their homes near the Everglades. They didn't live on the reservation, and they didn't live in grass-covered chickee huts, the way I imagined. Their house looked like any other suburban fortress in Miami, complete with a flat-screen TV and a stereo the size of a station wagon.

Jim, the man with the silver ponytail, represented the Tiger clan. He and his sons were supervising a controlled burn on one of their islands. That's when they discovered the bonfire.

"You kids are damn lucky we came along. Damn lucky. Especially you," he said, jerking his head at Haylie. "Could get an infection real easy out there." Jim bandaged her up. Turns out the bullet just grazed her skin. It may hurt like hell, but those types of scrapes always look messier than an actual puncture wound.

A tapestry stretched across the wall behind Jim's head. Beneath it, a big-boned woman in an Elvis T-shirt sat at the table, stringing plastic beads.

"For the tourists," she explained. "I tell 'em these necklaces are a hundred years old."

"My wife, Sarah, thinks she's funny," Jim said.

"*They're* funny because they believe me."

We settled on the floor, picnic-style, and gobbled leftover Chinese out of little paper cartons. Sebastian and the girls chowed down like they hadn't eaten in days. Alone in the corner, Brent stood back, stirring his tea with a chopstick.

"Pretty good death rate," Sebastian said. "Only a few egg rolls made it out alive."

"I need some Oompa Loompas to roll me out," Haylie said.

It felt like my bones had been chewed up and spit out. Every part of me hurt, especially on the inside.

"Are you hanging in there?" I asked my sister.

"Kinda sorta," she said, wincing. "As long as I don't breathe too hard. Oh, wait a sec." She pulled a cell phone out of her bag. "I think this is yours. I found it in the bushes before I saw you and..."

She looked away and handed it to me. The room spun.

"Is it on?" I managed to choke.

"I just checked to see if it still worked."

My fingers trembled as I punched the button to wake

up the screen and saw the three bars. There was nothing I could do.

Jim and the rest of the family headed for the kitchen and cleaned up. When I offered to help, they just waved me away.

Morgan nibbled a fortune cookie. "Happy birthday to me," she sang under her breath.

"What's your fortune say?" I asked.

"I don't know. I never look at them." She unfolded it slowly. "It says, Soft Drink."

"What?" Skully giggled.

"I'm just reading what it says. The Chinese word for 'soft drink' is *ke le*."

I shoved another egg roll in my mouth. "That's supposed to be your fortune?"

"What's yours say?"

I read, "Every person is the architect of their own future."

The girls laughed. Hard to believe, only hours ago, we were trapped in the burning swamp.

Morgan flipped the paper over. "Oh. Cool. It says my team will be very prosperous."

Brent threw his chopstick across the room. "You guys are a bunch of fools, sitting around, laughing with this freak."

Would this kid ever let up? Rage boiled up in me suddenly. "You're the freak. Who aims a gun at someone?"

He pointed at me. "Don't you get it?" he shouted at the girls. "As soon as this is over, he's going to narc us out."

Morgan squeezed my hand. "I trust him."

"Me too," Skully said.

The room went silent.

Brent turned to Sebastian and clapped him on the shoulder. "What about you, big guy?"

Sebastian frowned. "Aaron's always been cool with me. I mean, if he was going to do something bad, it would've happened already. Right?"

"Oh, my god. You people are idiots." Brent stormed out of the room.

Jim came back and asked, "What's his problem?"

"He's pissed at me," I said.

"Anger is a wasteful emotion," Jim said. "Why get angry at the past?"

"Easier said than done."

Jim sighed. "Who said life was easy?"

We camped on the living room rug. Jim was cool enough to let us use his land line to call our parents. As we waited to be picked up, the others conked out on the floor, but I stayed awake, listening to ice rattle in the freezer. I got up and went to the window. No pigeons stirring on the ledge. Just a broken flowerpot.

I stared out into the dark. I couldn't see anything without my glasses, not even trees. Just blurry nothingness. At that moment, my life felt just as empty.

My scraped-up arm was stinging, but not as badly as when Jim dumped a bottle of peroxide on it. I'd groaned as it fizzed and bubbled, and he called me a baby. I'd been called worse. On top of that, I'd lost the rubber band. I couldn't even remember how or when it happened. It was just gone.

I grabbed my cell phone and tried calling the lead officer. No response. I sent him a text message:

It's over.

Minutes passed.

Still no response.

This was really weird. He always had his phone. I went back to my blanket on the floor. Morgan had stretched out in one of those oversized cartoon T-shirts, which she'd borrowed from Jim's wife. It was Spiderman. I brushed the bangs out of her face and traced my finger along her body, following the slope of her back.

What was going to happen to us? Would she freak if I told her, "Look. I messed up big time. I can't stick around here anymore." Maybe I could apply for college next year. It was time I started living my own life. Doing what I wanted to do. Not that I had it figured out yet. I was just so tired of trying to please everybody else.

Carpe diem.

I got under the covers, but I still couldn't fall asleep. My Spidey senses were tingling. For a while, I tossed and turned. Just as the room started to brighten, I heard multiple footsteps scuffling outside the front door, and the dog began to bark.

The cops found us.

One text message. That's all they needed.

They thought this was the "take down" signal.

Shit.

I tried to shake Morgan awake, but she just mumbled something and rolled over.

"Let's go," I hissed.

She opened her eyes. "Aaron?"

The room shimmered. I wiped my eyes and tried to stay calm. "Get up. Please, just move. Goddamn it. You want to rot in jail?"

She still didn't get it. "Aaron, why are we going to jail?"

The door banged open and slammed against the wall. Somebody hollered a command. The room exploded with noise. The guy at the head of the line busted into the place and tossed in a "flash-bang," a harmless grenade meant to create confusion. And it did.

Morgan screamed as the foot soldiers dropped down, huddling in each corner of the room. They were dressed in riot gear: vests and shin pads, faces hidden under wasplike helmets.

Haylie knelt on the floor, clutching her head, as if fending off a nuclear bomb. The men kept telling her to stand with her arms in the air.

"Leave her alone. She's just a kid," I shouted, the words like an echo from the traffic stop months ago. But nobody listened. The dog wouldn't stop barking. Then Jim and Sarah were in the room and their mouths moved, but I couldn't understand what they were saying. I just saw their panic-stricken faces. Only Brent stood with no expression as the foot soldiers clamped the handcuffs over his wrists and herded him outside.

The girls crouched in their borrowed pajamas. I watched, in horror, as a foot soldier pointed his gun at Morgan and told her to "move, move, move."

I shoved my way between them.

"Get away from her," I yelled.

The foot soldier pushed me aside. Another one wrestled me against the wall and yanked back my arms. I could feel things tearing inside my muscles as the handcuffs tightened. The cold metal burned.

As he squeezed the cuffs tighter, I glanced at the faces of my friends, then slumped to the floor.

28 Sincerely/You

Status: SENT
To: LadyM
From: Metroid
Subject: Angel And The Jerk

You will probably hate me forever, but I wanted to write things down from my own perspective. I spent a lot of time, trying to explain what really happened.

I got the feeling nobody wanted to hear it.

Finch belongs in jail. So does Brent. Once the cops got hold of that video, those guys didn't have a chance. The judge could've thrown the book at you, but I stood up for everybody in court.

I stood up for you.

That's the truth.

If you were here in front of me, what would I do?

I'd take you down to the boat dock. We'd sit on that chimney by the hermit's house and dangle our feet in the tide. I'd kiss you, just as the rain clouds start to gather—charcoal smudges shaped like wings. No secrets between us. Just the water, which never stays still.

I kept all your drawings.

There's so much more I want to say.

I'm signing this letter, "Love," but I know you won't believe me.

Someday I hope you do.

Love,
Aaron

It thundered every day that following summer but barely ever rained. When it did, it was the hard kind of drizzle that burns your skin. I spent a lot of time skating in those downpours, as if it could soak through all my guilt and make me clean.

We moved back to Homestead after Mom got a job at the elementary down the street. "Band Aids and boo boos," she calls it. Then Haylie started her first year of high school. Kind of hard to believe. She's already bugging me to teach her how to drive. If she's extra nice, I'll let her borrow Dad's truck, now that it's fixed and there's primer over the graffiti. Once you learn stick, the rest is easy. At least, that's what Dad used to tell me.

I'm taking classes at Miami Dade. Nothing too hard-core. Just your basic community college stuff—biology, English comp, math for dummies. Still, I managed to sneak a photo class into my boring schedule. Dad would've laughed about that.

I'm trying to do better. Honestly, I am.

The cops helped me get things going. They wrote a letter of recommendation, once I earned my "good enough degree," the GED (There was no way I could go back to Palm Hammock after the arrests and court stuff.) Don't get me wrong. It's majorly weird, being in school again. When I walk down the hall, people stare. Maybe they read the news online. Or heard it on TV.

People talk about Finch like they knew him. Now that he's locked up, he's morphed into the stuff of legend. It already feels like forever ago, like it happened to someone I used to know. My name was kept secret. But secrets never last long, if you've got something to hide.

I don't want to hide anymore.

Not long after classes started, I was taking pictures for homework. We were supposed to do a self-portrait. The catch? (Yeah, with teachers, there's always a catch). You couldn't include yourself in the picture. At first I was like, How lame is that? The more I thought about it, the more it made total sense.

On Saturday, I drove to Coral Castle in search of

inspiration. The castle is just a bunch of rocks that some old guy named Ed carved into things like a heart-shaped table and pair of thrones. They say he did it for love. His girlfriend ditched him, but he never stopped hoping she'd come back.

I took Haylie along for the photo adventure. I even let her drive around the parking lot. Why not? She's always been my copilot.

We got out and headed toward the front gate, where a sign said: YOU WILL BE SEEING UNUSUAL ACCOMPLISHMENT.

"So he built this place all by himself?" Haylie asked. "Did he have magic powers or what?"

"He was probably some kind of insane genius," I said, aiming my camera at a lizard in the grass.

"Or maybe just insane."

While I blabbed about the levitating powers of magnets, I watched a group of people having a Kodak moment near the moon fountain. This one dude was trying to "plank" on the edge. That's when you stretch out, flat on your stomach, and someone takes a picture of you and posts it online. Pretty exciting, right?

His girlfriend kept telling him to "Hold still," but she couldn't stop laughing. Finally, they both gave up. He was making a big deal, like she had ruined his day or whatever, but I knew he was into it.

Something sparkled on the ground—a penny wedged in the dirt. It probably dropped out of the guy's pocket.

The girl reached for it, then looked at me, and if I really did have magic powers, I would've made myself invisible because that girl was Morgan.

Her hair was pulled back tight, swirled on top of her head like a pastry. I'd never seen her like that—in a tank top and leggings, as if any minute, she might bust out some ballet moves—her bare arms, the scars, right there.

The penny glinted in the sun.

Now I had two choices:

I could walk away. Or I could pick it up.

I started walking toward Morgan, like we were the only humans left on the planet.

"Aaron?" she said. Just my name.

"Do you know this guy?" asked her boyfriend, the planker.

"Yeah. I know him."

We stared at each other, holding the silence between us.

Morgan turned to her dude and said, "I need a minute, okay?"

He slunk off toward the gift shop. I could tell he wasn't cool with the idea of leaving us alone, but I had to give him props—he let us have some space. My sister was off in Haylie-land. It was just me and Morgan and the haunted rocks.

"You look good," I said.

"Thanks." She tucked a stray hair behind her ear. It killed me, the way something so small could bring back Morgan's everything. Around her neck, she wore an old-school, point-and-shoot camera.

"Still taking pictures?" Yeah, I was stating the obvious. What the hell was I supposed to say?

"It's my one and only superpower. Documenting reality."

"What kind of lens you got? It's a Holga, right?"

"Oh, I'm just messing around with it," she said. "I got the quad lens. It divides the picture, you know? So the frame is, like, split into four parts. Kind of cheesy, I guess."

"No, that sounds cool. There's always more than one way of looking at things."

"Yeah?"

"I mean, it's awesome that you're still doing art."

"My teacher says it's cheating. He says you're supposed to be 'making your own choices.'"

"But it's still your choice, right? You decide what to shoot."

She smiled. "I'll tell him you said that."

It felt so easy, talking to her again. Almost like we never stopped talking.

"Actually, I'm still bonding with this camera," she said. "My stepmom bought it for my graduation. It's pretty sweet, except you can't see the pictures before they're developed."

"True. But isn't it better, not knowing what comes next?" I asked, thinking of Mr. Pitstick, the way he used to go off about the past.

"Maybe," she said, dipping her hand in the fountain, where coins of all sizes caught the light.

"You still talk to Skully?" I asked.

"Sometimes," she said. "We take classes at the same

school, but it's like we're in different worlds. I think she's trying to reinvent herself. I just wish she wouldn't shut me out. We used to tell each other everything, you know?"

I did know.

We stood there, wiping our fists on our jeans, waiting to say all the things we hadn't said. Then Morgan kissed my cheek. The standard Miami greeting. I always thought it was so fake; this time, it was the most real thing she could do.

"Aaron, I read all your letters."

When she said it, I half-expected her to chew me out. Tell me I'm no good. Or worse. She read every word and didn't believe any of it. Instead, she untwisted her hair, letting it spill across her shoulders. She rolled the elastic over my wrist and, of course, it fit just right.

As she walked away, I couldn't look at her. On the ground was the dirty penny. I reached down and scooped it up.

"You can't go stealing other people's wishes."

My little sister had snuck up behind me.

"Here," she said, pressing a different coin into my hand. "Start over."

The quarter felt warm and solid. It wasn't new, but it shined, just the same.

I turned my back to the fountain.

Counted to three.

Then let go.

About the Author

Crissa-Jean Chappell (Miami, FL) is the award-winning author of *Total Constant Order* (Harper Teen). She is a professor of creative writing, and her reviews, short stories, and poems have appeared in many magazines.

Acknowledgments

Shout out to my fearless agent, Kate Lee, for believing in this book from the start. To my editor Brian Farrey-Latz, for your wise eyes and thoughtful insight. Big ups to Team Flux: Courtney Colton, Nicole Edman, and Steven M. Pomije.

Mucho hugs to the Chappell family, the Air Force brats, and especially my mom and dad for all your support. Jonathan, for reminding me that there is no ceiling. Harlan, who stayed on the phone all night. I love you guys!

Thanks to those who listened along the way: Candace Barbot, Houston Cypress (Otter Clan), Danielle Joseph, my epically amazing students, and Michna, who knows real street magic, including Aaron's levitation trick (made famous by David Blaine). Also helpful is Mary Dodge's article, *Juvenile Police Informants: Friendship, Persuasion, and Pretense*, and its exploration of Chad's Law, which was created to protect teenage informants. I am incredibly grateful to many people who must remain unmentioned, but were invaluable to my research. This book could not exist without you.